A BURIED TREASURE

ELIZABETH MADOX ROBERTS

THE GREAT MEADOW

JINGLING IN THE WIND

MY HEART AND MY FLESH

THE TIME OF MAN

UNDER THE TREE (*verse*)

A BURIED TREASURE

ELIZABETH MADOX ROBERTS

1931
The Literary Guild
New York

A greatly abridged rendering of this work appeared in Harper's Magazine, December 1929 and January 1930.

TO

IVOR ROBERTS

A BURIED TREASURE

I

WHEN THE SUNLIGHT CAME STRAIGHT THROUGH THE southern doorway and made a square block of light on the kitchen floor, Philadelphia Blair, called Philly, knew that the noon of day was approaching. Now the sun was printing its noon mark within the door and she found that her woodbox was empty of large burning pieces. She had cut the summer cabbage into quarters for cooking, and she leaned low over the woodbox to stir the fine dust there, looking for small kindling sticks. Out of the sediments arose the odors of rotting cedar wood and pine mixed with the more faint odors from hundreds of burnings of beech or locust or poplar. Small gray wood mites crept about in the disturbed dust and hurried away to shelter under the minute chips, as if fine particles

3

of wood had come to life in the scarcity of the bin. Philly stirred the dust about, being amused to see life buried there, having forgotten for a long while the dust in the bottom of the woodbox and forgotten that wood mites live by eating it.

She leaned low over the woodbox and laughed softly at the creatures she saw scurrying about there. They paddled away on their dry quick legs to find shelter from the light and from her eyes, as if life for them were precious and they would flee to keep it. All of them had run into the darkness of the undisturbed dust where her prodding stick had not been, but another reach of her thrusting hand and she had turned up their hiding and they were running further, here and there, finding newer shelter. She was pleased at seeing the wood mites and she laughed lightly as she knelt beside the bin. She began to think of them as being like men and women, her neighbors, and to name them by such names, as "There goes Sam Cundy, the big cock-sure one," or "This-here little smart one in a fidget is Callie Webster." They were all gone safely to shelter again, their heads drawn under the dust, but one turn of her poker through the mass and their small universe was set into its day of wrath again. She might at any moment shovel the dust of the woodbox into her stove and burn it, making a brief lake of fire in which their day of wrath would end.

Stirred again, and the whole of the Elk Creek country, her neighbors, herself, her husband Andy Blair, here in the little, were fleeing over the torn earth. She gave them her pity and her faint scorn, hating them that their fate should be fixed and their way of life meager. They climbed crumbling bluffs of the torn world and sank again into an abyss she devised for them with her hand. They labored upward over tottering dust to fall at the top when her hand went among them. Since hate was quickly spent, a rush of newer pity washed over her, and, being surprised by this, she stayed her hand. She blinked her eyes to disperse their tears and left the creatures to their poor security, for all of them were now sheltered under the fine chippy dust. She went away from the woodbox altogether.

She passed through the sitting-room or parlor which lay just before the kitchen. A third room, at the left of the parlor, had a stairway that mounted to rooms above. The upper rooms were low under the slant of the roof. From the upper north window she looked out over the barn enclosures and the garden, and she cried out Andy's name, her mind on the empty wood bin. When her survey of the near-lying places did not reveal him, she knew that he must be away at some remote part of the farm patching a fence.

Searching again, she found only a few splinters and a bit of trash at the woodpile. The word "woodpile" but named a place, and not a heap or lot of anything. She slammed the two kitchen doors, north and south, and went out in anger, stepping quickly through the hot sunlight.

"No wood in the woodpile," she said; "empty it is. A man that lets the woodpile get empty is a mighty poor provider, I always said."

She went forward through the bright hot air, thinking a picture: Andy driving homeward across the pasture with a load of knotty sticks and logs in the wagon, wood for the woodpile. There was no such appearance. The pasture was bare, even of feeding cattle. She looked back once at the small brown house which was withered by the sun and swollen by the rains of many seasons, and she saw that it drooped slightly toward the earth, the roof bowed at the corners. The shut door was blank against the summer light, and the hens about the door followed her in a concern for corn, but she brushed them from her path with a windy apron and thought again in anger of the dinner that stood uncooked.

At the end of the garden she climbed a low fence and went up through an open pasture to the brow of the hill where Andy worked. His bent back seemed very tall behind his patched coat as she mounted the hill, and his regard for the fence seemed to spread over the whole front of the hill, as if a fence were more than food for the mouth and more than fire for cooking. He made a slow elaborate care of the fence, delaying each act and making each important, and she stood by watching but saying nothing. When he had patched at the wires for five minutes she said:

"I reckon you're not a hungry man. Dinnertime right here at us and the summer cabbage on the stove in cold water, waiten to boil. A man-person is a contrarious sort, the best you'd find, but you are a poor make-out-like man as ever I did see. You can go hungry till you get home some firewood."

He slowed his acts to meet these accusations, making a great matter of the fence, deliberating on the set of a wire and the space of the staples. When he had established the importance of the fence with the last blow of his hammer he took his ax from the ground and climbed over the fence, going a little way into his cornfield. He began to dig at an old stump to break it apart, making firewood. Philly went over the fence and presently she began to gather the pieces of wood into her apron.

As she stooped to take up the wood she saw the wood mites again, here running away from the sunlight, crawling in and out of the rotted wood, darting over the loose fibers of the broken stump on their small quick legs. Then she saw the world outside, beyond the stump, viewed it from under her looped-up apron, and saw it reversed and enlarged in her bent vision, strange, upside-down, and remote in its far-reaching spaces. She remembered a story of an old war and remembered that a small battle had been fought near this place, stories of people fleeing from their homes, of parts of missiles turned up by the plow. She dropped her apron a few inches and blotted out the wide strange world beyond, returning to her familiar medium, the minute and the near. The old soil about the stump gave back withered empty odors and the rotting flakes of wood fell softly from her hands. There were wood mites hurrying into the darker chambers of the sticks. She knew them as the same she had uncovered indoors in the leavings of her woodbox. They would turn and creep swiftly away when they were uncovered. They were to her now as of the same substance as the wood; they were of the same kind as that through which they crept. They were continually there; even burnt with the sticks they were always back wherever wood was rotting.

"What's taken the dog?" Andy asked. "I never see the dog in such a swivet before."

The dog had come to the stump while she gathered her apron full of the scattered wood. The hound was clawing at the base of the stump and making quick nervous motions about the roots, drawing back and leaping forward. Andy dug into the roots with his ax, scarcely able to brush the dog aside, and his tool struck some hard metal surface. Philly turned away, ready now to go with her burden, to prove her indifference to anything he might find in the field, but she saw the dog leaping and barking about the ruined stump as she went evenly toward the fence and made ready to climb over it. Andy cried out with a sharp phrase of oath or imprecation and he dug into the stump with hurried blows, trying to push the dog aside.

"It's a pot of gold," he said, his voice hoarse with confused pleasure and distress. Without ceasing to hack at the root-wood he called toward Philly, "A pot! It must be money! What else?"

Philly came back, carrying her burden, and she

stood deridingly by, ready to laugh when the object came to hand, storing her laughter. "An old plow-iron," she said. "Somebody's old broken plow."

"It's a kettle," Andy said. "See the bulge on the side here?" He stopped the work of his ax to point out the shape of the object that was hidden, drawing lines in the air with his sweeping hand.

"It's a kettle maybe, but what would a kettle be under a stump for?"

"That's the part I can't answer. That's why I say it's money. Gold money, what else?"

"It could be a plowshare, turned at the end, bent maybe."

"Take care, take care outen the way," Andy said, speaking wearily, as if he hardly knew what she had been saying. He began to dig again and Philly stood aside. She remembered the cold dinner pot in her kitchen and she wavered for a moment between the wish to make it boil and the wish to see Andy dig out the buried object. He lashed with the ax as if he were young again. He did not want the iron under the ground to be a plowshare, and she waited to see what he would do when the old iron piece came out of the earth and out of the roots that bound it. He would kick it aside and say that it might easily have been a kettle, that the bulge at the side had made it look like a pot. She was still smarting under the neglect of her woodbox and she wanted him to wait for his dinner until he should be hungry for it. She held the sticks of wood so that the burden rested on her hip, to ease the soft part of her body from the pressure, and she said:

"I reckon you need a plow in a bad way. And iffen you don't need it I can use it to prop shut the little hen-house door, so loose on its hinge it wants to flop open any hour of the day or night. I always said one hinge is not enough to a door anyway."

"It's a pot, no matter," Andy said, hacking more deeply. He caught his breath as if he were spent by his hard blows. "A kettle it is, no matter."

"I can use a kettle too," Philly said. "Rub it smooth with wood ashes and lye and it's fitten to cook in, or if that don't clean it I can still use it to prop shut the door. Fill it full to the top with rocks to make it heavy. . . . I can use a kettle in case you don't want one to hold the axle grease for the wagon wheels. . . . Even let it be a pot and I'll find use a-plenty for it to make it worth your sweat. . . ."

The ax broke away the rotting wood and parted the earth, letting the iron out. It was indeed a vessel. Andy freed a rusty handle and broke the vessel from the hard earth that packed it. He tore the stump completely and made an entire wreck of it. He called on Philly for help, and she dropped her firing and tugged with him at the vessel. It came free at last and they raised it to the ground and broke away the clods. Under their hands stood a small iron pot, a cooking vessel of average size. It was covered over with an iron lid that was cemented into place by the clay, but Andy pried it away with his ax. Inside were gold and silver coins, tarnished with disuse, but clear to see in the bright light. As Philly looked at them they swam in a dim fog of unbelief, stared out of view and scarcely accepted, but Andy made broken speeches of prayer and good feeling, swearing that he had never seen the like of this and naming God with praise, naming his own good luck with admiration. The blackened coins were swimming in and out of her view and she felt a sickness at the top of her stomach, but Andy was crying out:

"Philly, Philly, we're a rich man and woman now. We're rich beyond anything we ever dreamed. I got no idea how rich we might be. Oh, God be praised!"

"How do I know it's money?" she said. "Even if I touch it, how do I know it's a right kind?"

She walked three steps away and looked about at the far hillside, coming back suddenly in order to surprise the pot, if it were still there. She walked about, looking down into the mouth of it where Andy had stirred the coins a little with his fingers. She had not yet touched the gold.

"Bless God!" Andy said, as if he were religious, speaking over and over, and he made an oath of damnation for himself if he were not a man of luck. He babbled with pleasure and bound himself to prosperity with oath after oath. "Put your hand inside and feel," he said to Philly. "Feel it with your hands and then you won't say 'maybe' and 'what if' and such-like nonsense. Put in your hand and feel."

Philly could not believe. "It might not be real money, fitten to spend here in this country. Or we might wake up and find it's all in a dream."

"Take a-hold," Andy said. They carried the kettle to the fence and lifted it over. A hot wind seemed to blow through the bright sunlight and the journey to the fence seemed long and full of peril. Beyond the fence Andy flung Philly's apron over the pot and left her to guard it while he went back to the stump where he took away the broken wood and looked into the hole for more wealth, but he found none and, having dug the earth about the stump until it fell into clods, he closed the hole he had made. The pot seemed real then to her, as if it might stay, but the day seemed strange, as if it were free to go or to turn into some other. Andy came back to the treasure and they stopped again to talk of the wonder they had found and to ask each other what they had best do with it and how it came to them and whose it might have been in the beginning. Andy had inherited the land from his father, who had inherited it in turn; but he could not remember that there had ever been any story of lost money in the family.

"My pap was a well-doen man," he said, standing over the pot, "in nobody's debt as ever I heard. But he wasn't a man to put by money in a kettle. He'd set store by a bank if he had money to save. Bless God, did you ever hear tell of a man had so much luck?"

Walking with Andy, carrying a pot of gold across the pasture, she was thrust out of all that she had known formerly. She had never thought to be doing this. The pot went back of everything she knew and made there a new beginning. It went back of the first knowledge she had, back of all the first fragrance she had gathered. It spread widely through the present, herself now, walking strangely across the pasture. She was confused that this should happen to her. They set the kettle down and stood over it to talk. Walking slowly forward again she thought of the old war and of the world as she had seen it from under her looped-up apron. The house seemed far, the roof lines strange when they were seen, the whole too vivid and sharp in her sight, the well stones too clear to see, hard under foot. The guineas in the barn lot were crying "quatrack," making a high thin scream, as if they, with the kettle, were strangers. During the old war a battle had been fought not far away—the crack of guns and the shouting of men, men hurrying farther away, men running along the roads swiftly on horseback. This was hers through hearsay. Herself, walking now over the stones that lay before the rear door of the house, was more strange than the war.

"Will we ring the farm bell and call in all the neighbors?" Andy asked.

"We could," she said. "Seems almost we might be bound to."

"We best wait a spell till we see what 'tis," he said, after he had thought quietly for a little. "We best wait . . ."

At the house they spread the money on the floor and counted the coins. These were gold and silver pieces of American coinage, all bearing dates earlier than 1860. When the pieces were counted the sum was found to be something above nineteen hundred dollars. Andy laid the coins in rows, kind beside kind, and he arranged them in graduated array or he rallied them in even files, counting them again, and his breath became short and quick with passion as he made the sum mount. Philly saw new manners spread over him, and she heard new joys surge up in his voice. He talked of what he would do with the treasure to keep it safe, or he fitted it back into the pot and knew again the joy of finding it, a cat recapturing its mouse. Will-o'-the-wisp money lay on their floor to be counted over, to be realized again and again, to be re-created over and over. Elusive gold had come to them out of an old stump. Andy became the person she had held in mind as the man to whom she had been wedded for thirty years, the person who arose within to answer her despairing question, "Did I marry a lout, a poor miser of a skinflint named Andy?" He became the reply; he became Mr. Blair, a man seen from outside the farm, from a long distance, from the county seat, or from a little town toward the north where she sometimes went to buy. The storeman there had never seen Andy. He gave him great honor, inquiring particularly after his likes and dislikes, creating him from her own particular wants and from her quick tongue. Now this one, created long ago and preserved in the myth of the storeman, was speaking, an easy, confiding happiness in his face:

"Somebody buried this enduren the war," half whispering.

"Enduren the war, yes," he whispered.

Philly fingered the trash that was left in the kettle. There were strange bits of broken ends of things she could not define and she began to take the fragments apart, finding a name for a sort if she could. There were bits of thread or rags and a few small pebbles and there was a lump of some other substance which she picked carefully to pieces. In her fingers, as her eyes peered close, it was a small roll of old silken cloth tied together with a rotting thread which she peeled off bit by bit. The cloth fell away to dust and rotted lint, and inside were two pale round shapes that rolled together in the palm of her hand, two clear stones that caught the light of the room in a faint opalescent glow. They were of the size of two small grains of wheat, and they quivered lightly to-

gether. "They are two pearls," she said, holding them near to her face. "They are like the kind I saw once in a pin Verdie Stoner used to wear on her breast before she lost her power to hear clearly, only in the pin were three and ne'er one so large as this."

Andy looked at them, taking them into his hand, and he searched the trash in the bottom of the pot carefully, fingering each bit near his eyes, but there were no other jewels. These two had been tied into a bit of silken cloth and laid into the kettle with the silver and gold.

"They are fine jewel stones," Andy said, laying them carefully back into the pot. Philly took them into her hand again and wondered at their clear roundness.

"They are two pearls. They are not diamonds, I know. Diamonds are clear like glass. These are rich pearls, fitten for a queen, but smaller, maybe. They are a fine sight to see. In a pin they would make a fine show on a woman's breast."

"It's almost more than you can believe, that there would be two jewels, even small ones, in the kettle," Andy whispered, leaning low over the pearls. "Civil War times, I reckon. Somebody buried the pot when that tree was a sprout, and I dug it outen a hickory stump."

"Your old pappy never once judged there was a kettle of money and two pearls buried in his old worn-out field, did he? You don't reckon it ever belonged to your old grand-daddy, do you?" she asked. The Blairs had been a fine race. Making no great show with money or with land, they had still been proud. Having no visible signs of finery, they had been fine somehow in spite of whatever they lacked. "You reckon it would be a Blair kettle?"

Andy shook his head and turned back to finger the money. "I couldn't say. There wasn't any hearsay of a kettle in the house, either side o' the family." He was a gentle, reasonable man, leaning over the coins, a man well liked by all the neighbors and a man of dignity. His thin hair was hanging in one long lock, forward from his brow as he bent over the pot. The rims of his eyes were red, as they always were, and there were little lobes and spots on his eyeballs that seemed to keep momentary company with his eyes, as if they were there only for a short time and would be gone from the next eyes she looked at. His face was cut with innumerable wrinkles and his mouth was loose-hanging with the downward sweep of his body.

"These-here coins all got inside the pot before

war times," he said. "Many is the time my pap, he plowed that field and set his feet down in two feet of this-here money. Pap as poor as Job's own turkey all his enduren life. The man that owned the pot as likely as not killed in the war. I am undoubtedly a master hand to have good luck. Did ever you see such luck, Philly?"

"What'll you buy with the money?" she asked. "What could we buy to show the world we found a pot of gold and silver?"

"I always was a master hand to find things," he said. "Good luck seems to come my way. I'm the best-off man in these parts, as apt as not, right now."

"A new roof to the house, maybe," she said. "A new roof on the hen-house. The old one leaks as bad as any roof I ever did see. The water runs down through the little holes where the nails used to be and it makes a little shower again inside the hen-house. The hens, they see a right hard time in a wet season."

"And now I'm a well-doen man, as well-doen as e'er other man on Elk Creek, take all as they come."

"I'll tell you what I'd like to get, outen the pot of money, Andy," she said, in her mind speaking to Mr. Blair, her voice almost whispering, "a little something for Imogene. My own cousin's girl-baby she was, and look what a life she leads with her pap and those boys, her brothers, as close a set as ever you did see. Too stingy to let Imogene marry Giles Wilson."

She began to think of a wedding for Imogene, a bountiful supper and people at hand. She had come into a strange world, and all her fiber seemed to be touching strangeness. The seat on which she rested seemed to bear her up in a strange way, and she remembered the summer cabbage still standing uncooked on the stove. The morning had crawled strangely past noon, no dinner being set on the table. She decided swiftly that she would give Imogene a wedding.

"We'll give Imogene a wedden," she said. "A big wedden with fried oysters, maybe, from town. I always think it's nice to have a wedden if a couple marry. Weddens are so pleasant. I just love weddens."

"A master hand to have luck, I always was," Andy followed his own. "The only man on Elk Creek that's not in debt, bad crop years no matter, but borrow money I would not. I says, 'I'll starve first.'"

"And about near starve we did," she said, going out of the strangeness of the day, looking backward. "I recall days we had ne'er a thing but mush bread to eat. And dry summers, the cow dry and no sour milk to make with. Mush bread and cured meat, maybe, and a little fruit I had canned for sweet on a Sunday."

"And now I'm the best-off man in these parts. Did ever you hear of another had my luck, up and down this-here creck?"

"It's a fine thing to find in a stump," she said. "It'll buy us . . . what'll it buy us, Andy Blair?"

"It's a fine thing for a man to find on his land. What other man did you ever know found a kettle of gold and silver in his cornfield? I always was a lucky man. I'll keep the money inside the pot for a spell. I recollect I heard Lester Rudds say once, 'Andy Blair has always got all the luck.' You recollect times you've heard that said? I always was favored a heap. I don't know what 'tis about me draws all the luck my way."

"I never see so much luck you had before this," she said.

A tall, slow-moving man, who might at any instant become elegant, stood as a fog around Andy and then went out quickly. She left the little chair where she had been sitting and walked about the room. The creature on the floor beside the money pot was a hungry. long-boned, crook-jointed man, wanting only two or three things in the world. He was unwilling to do anything or to think anything without her, was always telling her what he did, running in to tell her if a pig broke through the fence or if a tool was broken. He wanted her to be continually an extended part of himself, to help out his consciousness. She walked about in the end of the room, near the fireplace, and he was muttering of his good luck. He was telling of his good fortune, a happy slobber running at the corners of his mouth. She sensed the soggy, flabby, sour, unwilling and crooked rottenness of lean flesh and the little mouths of the skin out of which came mean, ill-odored vapors. She saw him, naked and crooked-shaped, bending forward. Her senses were hard and set, to expel him. When he moved his shoulder, bending forward, she disliked the motion he made as she would hate the movements of a mange-eaten beast.

She sat down toward the doorway and began to look scornfully at his past, searching it for any good fortune. She held it up in jointed, terse sentences and broke it into fragments. She spoke more softly as her power mounted and her scorn grew.

"Recollect the time you spilled the corn in the creek?" she said. "Spilled a whole wagon-load in swollen flood water. Again, you recollect the time a white-trash traveler greened you out of your work-nag? You act so like white-trash yourself, folks would think you came from a white-trash set, but I know better. I always had it in mind I married a Blair." Good luck stood far apart from Andy then, and she drove it farther, recounting. "Recall the time you dug a well and didn't find so much as a damp spot underground?"

She reached to the mantel and found there a little twig she had broken from a wild-cherry tree. When she had broken a small stick from the twig she peeled back the bark to make a little brush which she dipped into her snuff can. The brush came out of the can heavily tasseled with the fine brown powder of the tobacco, and this she placed in her mouth beside her lower teeth, for a consolation. The savor spread mildly through the nerves of her mouth and soon it engendered a soft and delicate laughter at the base of her tongue. She spat a little of the brown mixture into the fireplace and sat quietly apart.

"What'll you buy with some of the money?" she asked finally.

"I'll keep all inside the pot for a spell," he answered. "It's a fair sight to see in the pot and a

surprise to your eye every time you cast it that
way. We'll keep all in the pot until we tell all the
neighbors what we found and let all have a look."
He was humbled, but he kept to his determined
way, saying little now. "We'll keep it in the pot,
and the pearls inside the pot too," he said.

"We'll have a surprise party and invite all our
kin. We'll invite maybe a small sprinklen of outside folks too, maybe Callie Webster and Ed Sims
and the Triggs and the Whites. And we'll show
them what a fortune we found against a stump in a
cornfield," she said. Andy was leaning low over
the kettle wiping at the corners of his mouth with
the back of his hand. The pot seemed to be a fine
thing then, beyond knowing about, as if one would
have to lean near to it to keep it close at hand.

She was in a gay humor, her little snuff stick
hanging at the corner of her lips. She could trust
Andy to keep a firm hold on the treasure, to know
it entirely, silver and gold and precious stones,
and how many of each kind were in the vessel.
Little was required of her and she began to enjoy
her part in the ownership of it. She rocked slowly
to and fro, filled with unspent laughter. "We'll
have a party and tell what we found," she said.
"Let Bonnie White and Robbie May Rudds and
Effie Trigg, let all bring their sweethearts indoors

for a spell. Let 'em come indoors and not be out
in the bushes, two and two, a-holden each other
till night is half over. Let all come indoors and wit-
ness what we found under a stump. I'll stop for a
little spell themselves from talken love-talk and
kissen in dark corners under lilac bushes, and out
on the road, pretenden they're a-goen somewheres.
I'll have a party now right off whilst the moon is
towards the full and they can walk home afterwards in the sunset of the moon. They'll all come,
as hearty as life itself, as if they're fitten to last
forever, and as if love-talk is a new kind they only
discovered this year. We'll ask can they find under
a lilac bush or a hackberry any better kind 'n we
found under a stump."

She named a half dozen others she would invite. "Callie will be plumb beside herself to
know what the surprise is." She thought then to
hurry some of the money out of the pot, to have
all their neighbors in to view it at one time. Andy
listened with delight when she told about the
party and he took pleasure in the thought of
a public announcement. "I'll not make a long-
winded speech," he cried out. "I'll come straight
down to facts. I'll say, 'Kinfolks and neighbors,
look what I found in my cornfield. A kettle of gold
money and silver, and two precious stones. Come

up all and have a look.' " His pride was restored in the thought of himself as having something to disclose. " 'Look what I found in my cornfield,' I'll say, off-handishly."

"I must wash your shirt with the little blue flowers," Philly said. "I'll wash tomorrow early in the morning."

"And Hez Turner," Andy named another. "Won't he be in a fidget to know what's to tell? Sing and pray over it, iffen you don't watch."

"Old Hez, he'll turn the surprise party into a chance to pray and preach. Maybe we better not invite Hez. We won't. Church is the place to preach and pray in, but the churches won't let old Hez inside to preach, hardly to pray even."

"We'll leave old Hez out," Andy said. "Let him find out the good news from some that came. He'd be sure to preach and pray right over the kettle iffen he's let."

"I think as much and the same," Philly said, agreeing at every point.

"I don't favor to invite Hester Trigg, Joe Trigg's widow," Andy continued after a little.

"We couldn't leave her out and invite the rest. I'm surprised to hear you say a word against Hester. She's bound to be invited. Why don't you favor to invite her?" Philly asked.

"She's a widow woman," Andy said, after he had thought a little. "She's a widow."

"Would that be a reason to leave her out?"

"I never liked widow women. Not iffen they've got it in head to marry again."

"She's a stout, hearty, well-set-up woman, pink cheeks and a little out of breath. Married twice already and outlasted both. She's a fine hand to cook and sew. Two children is all she's got, and they both married. Why wouldn't she marry again?"

"Once ought to content a woman."

"We can't leave her out, no matter."

"I don't favor much to invite her," Andy returned to his first opinion, letting pass his prejudice against widows. He was fingering the gold again, leaning low over it. "Iffen you say come, though, she can come. I won't say no to her. I don't care whe'r she comes or stays."

"We won't say what the surprise party is about. We'll just say there is a surprise and won't they like to come and see for themselves."

"That's what. We won't name the surprise. We'll just say come and see. It'll be a surprise then for a fact."

"I don't reckon a kettle full of money would ever enter in e'er head to be named, of all the lot we'd invite here. Do you think e'er one would think to name a pot of money?"

"I wouldn't trust Callie to handle the money too freely. Callie has right light fingers sometimes. I wouldn't trust Callie too far. I never heard it said Callie stole anything, but I always took notice her fingers are light."

"Callie can make black appear white, with her smooth tongue. I wouldn't trust Callie too far with a kettle of gold neither. It's her tongue is light, you mean, Andy. I wouldn't go so far a piece as to say Callie would take with her fingers, but she'd make it seem as if it ought to be somebody else's kettle."

"And I'll let it be known I already counted the pieces," Andy said, taking caution, "and let it be reported I know how many are in the pot. Iffen any is gone you can search all the women before they go out."

"We better not say where we found it," Philly said, becoming cautious too. "We'll say we dug it up but we won't show the place."

"I'm more uneasy," Andy said, "they might take the money outen the pot whilst we're not by to see. We can't stand by all day and watch the kettle. What would we do enduren the time we want to go outdoors?"

"We'll give a prize to the one that can name what the surprise is. We'll give one piece of silver to whoever can guess the surprise before we bring it out to show. Then we won't bring it out before everybody is about ready to start for home."

Andy sat, his arms resting on the top of the kettle, and he leaned heavily, guarding the pot while he eased himself. They were both tired now, and they asked each other where they would keep the money. It seemed safe only as it lay out under Andy's outstretched arms.

"Will we invite Johnnie Roundtree?" Philly asked. "I hear he's taken radio machines to sell."

"I heard so too. He sold already tombstones and fruit trees and beehives. He takes orders for four kinds now."

"We better not invite him," Philly said.

"It's said he ordered a tombstone for Giles Wilson's old pappy that's dead last year. When it came, by some mistake they sent it marked wrong. It's said he did, for a fact, try to get Giles Wilson to take a beehive, to satisfy the bill, in place of the wrong-marked stone. To use for a beehive though, not to put up over the grave, you understand."

"We better not invite Roundtree," Philly said again.

"We won't," Andy said. "Word about the kettle might get into the radio machine. It stands to reason iffen you can hear people talk in Texas and New York the people in New York and Texas can hear what you say again. It might get out a long piece about the pot that way."

Philly leaned down and looked into the kettle out of which the strange air seemed to arise. In the pot there was an old air musty with dry rottenness. Beyond this rot lay the little coins, and the silver looked much like the gold because of the blackening tarnish. Andy took a large goldpiece from the pot and began to polish it on his leg, but he laid it down slowly and lifted his head to look at Philly with a far-gaze in his eyes.

"Philly," he said, "you know what this kettle of gold recalls to my mind? It recalls the time I heard a voice speak outen the air. I walked along the road, a cold day in spring, nobody else by, and I heard a voice."

"I recollect the voice you told about. I recall there was a voice spoke to you. I don't recollect what it said, though."

"I walked along the road, nobody near me, and I heard a voice:

> Andrew Blair
> Come here. . . .

The voice spoke the words in a slow way, long
drawn out. I recall I could hardly sit still in my
seat or relish my food all day afterward."

"It's a pity the voice didn't say where to come
to." They were quiet, thinking of the voice. It was
Andy who had heard, not the elegant, knowing
gentleman, but the halting, stubborn, fearful,
bony, weather-seasoned one. He had a gentle sort
of pride in the voice, for it was a wonder he had
experienced privately. He stared at the floor while
he seemed to be listening, and his lock of hair
fell forward, his mouth slightly opened. It was
strange to her that he should have heard any such
thing; she had never had such a thing happen to
her. It was past belief. He was for a moment a
stranger. They were weary, leaning together over
the kettle, their hands on the upper edge. She
talked of the mystery of the kettle, and she thrust
her fingers into it to lift the gold, bringing it back
to mind. Then she looked up quickly and said:

"Then we'll afterwards, after the party, give
Imogene a wedden. I'd like a heap to see Imogene
marry with a big supper."

"After the surprise is over," Andy said. "One
at a time is all I can hold in head. Afterward, why
maybe we might favor Imogene a little, for a fact
we might."

They considered places in which to hide the kettle, trying several before they were satisfied with a place. Down inside the organ it seemed safe, shut away into the dusty cabinet among the reeds and bellows pipes. But Andy distrusted the organ, fearing that it might give forth some revealing sound, for the pot crowded the inner part of the instrument and pressed on the bellows. Taken from the organ it was placed in the chimney, hung well above the line of vision even if one sat near the fireplace. It seemed secure there, the hearth being without fire now that the weather was warm, and it stayed there for a night. But uneasiness followed it there, and it was placed in the little cubbyhole in the room upstairs. Then the coins were brought out of the pot, a few at a time, and they were rubbed until they shone, scoured with wood ashes. This work required the whole of a day.

The land outside seemed vague now, diffused in Philly's thought, the kettle being now the right measure of the world. The opinions their neighbors would hold of it, if they knew, came back upon her and shaped again and again her mind in its delight and pride and fear, and she weighed the opinion of this one and that, seeing the kettle as Ronnie Rudds would see it, as Hester Trigg,

as Sam Cundy or Bud Stoner or Eliza White. Each
such opinion shaped it anew in her thought so
that, even now, while none shared her knowledge
but Andy, the pot had about it a shape beyond
itself, a continually shifting vapor of shared delight and awe and inquiry.

She thought frequently of Imogene, her young
cousin. Imogene was unlike herself, being tall and
quiet. Philly rubbed the gold coins with the gritty
ashes of the wood fires, and she washed them later
in a bowl of water. Sitting on the floor of the
upper room to scour the gold, a pleasant breeze
blowing into the room from the sugar trees outside
and Andy sitting near to hand her the pieces and
to rub them afterward with a piece of soft flannel,
she saw the coins become bright beneath her
fingers. Andy would mutter his pleasure, "They
are a fair sight to see now. . . . See, Philly, inside
the pot. . . . It surely is a sight to delight your
eyes. . . ." Philly's thought went back to Imogene, seen going up and down her father's house
lifting vessels, making food ready, putting food by
for winter, making the fire under the kettle. She
had been a small girl only last week, it seemed,
but when Philly counted backward, placing the
years with a happening for each one, she found
what time had passed.

"I thought I heard somebody walk on the step-rocks outside the door," Andy said, listening.

It was not a footfall. It was one of those strange sounds that come from nowhere, Philly said, after she had listened closely and had recalled what noise had been heard. The sound had not been that of a footstep, but rather of some vessel being set on a table in a kitchen. Thinking again of Imogene she saw her strong white hands moving quickly about. She walked up and down the house and the porches in a jog-trot, a sort of even dance, up and down, no end to it, always the same. When she was a small child her father had made a great pet of her. He would want her when he went to the field and he would carry her before him on the horse when he rode out to his farther farm to inspect his cattle. She was unlike herself, Philly, in everything, being tall and meek, even-spoken. When her mother died she had taken the place in the house. Philly counted back, naming event after event; Imogene had been fifteen, just about to grow tall, just about to become a girl among the other girls with things to giggle about, with visits to other girls' houses. She lived two miles away along the highroad after it forked, one way going east and the other north and west. She was seen in the eastern direction. Her hands were soft in spite of the work they were always doing, because they had a healthy moisture of their own. The last time Philly had gone there Cundy had made it clear he did not want her about. She could scarcely go to see Imogene again.

"I think I hear sounds below," Andy said. "Are the guinea-hens in a fidget, do you think?"

Philly listened carefully and she said she did not think the guineas were disturbed. They were not screaming.

"The guinea-hens are good fore-tellers," she said, "as good as doorbells. You can depend a heap on the guineas to let you know if anybody is about to come."

Andy leaned low over the coins to wipe each one, looking at it closely to be sure that all the tarnish was gone. Philly, seeing him thus careful, rubbed harder at the coin, continuing her inner musings. All the girls Imogene's age were pairing off with the young men. Philly remembered Imogene then as a baby, before she had hidden her body away. The women were saying now that Giles Wilson stopped to see Imogene whenever he passed along the road. Philly leaned low over a gold coin, rubbing it carefully, looking at the picture on the face of it, her mind in a dream. Imogene was like herself, being different in many

things, and while Philly rubbed the small goldpiece until it was clean, she felt as if she were the
same, identical with Imogene, as if the turn of her
hand and the pressure of her fingers on the little
rag that cleaned the gold of tarnish were Imogene's own. Then a passion arose within her, a
clear and swift determination to make a better
way of life for Imogene, to make her free to have
something for herself, to give her the pleasure of a
lover.

"What are the guineas a-doen now?" Andy
asked. "Can you hear because your ears are
sharper? . . . Can you hear whe'r they're in a
stir?"

There was no sound outside but the twittering
of the little bird that lived somewhere back of the
high tulip tree of the hen-yard, and the rush of
the south wind through the leaves of the trees.
Identical with Imogene, Philly dreamed forward a
pleasant story. All the other girls had their play-
parties when they sat out in the dew under the
lilac bushes with their sweethearts. It was a very
good way, she thought, turning several opinions
about, although their mothers avoided knowing
that they did this and withheld opinions. One
could turn around and around again on this
thought. Everything was hush and no and what-

of-it with the women, and change the subject to some other matter. The girls were in a way right and in a way cautious. But a boy might be a good lover and not make a good provider. And again he might not turn out to be the loving kind nor a good provider either. It was best not to care too much over it one way or the other. Let come what comes. One could turn around in seven different opinions over the case and there would still be a man at the other end of the string with his crotchets and habits and his little stingy ways, or his bad sense. She gave it up, but came back to it again immediately. All the circumstances around Imogene were different from those about the other girls, and the lilac bushes had little to do with her case. A man who would go past her father's sharp temper and his threats would be a good kind without the lilac bushes to sit under, and the hackberry bushes out along the road. Imogene was divided from all the others, standing taller and being more shy and restrained.

"What are the guineas about now, Philly? . . ." Andy's voice. "Can you hear iffen they are in a racket? . . ."

When the last coin was rubbed all were laid within the pot. Then Philly found a fine piece of white linen that was soft and old, and she tore from it a little square to make a wrapping for the two pearls. She gathered the corners of the small square together and tied the top with a little thread, making a very small pouch. Then Andy took this from her hand and he laid it carefully on the top of the coins inside the pot. The vessel was set again inside the cubbyhole of the upper room, well hidden under a pile of quilts.

On the second day after the finding of the treasure Imogene came tapping on the door and calling from without. She had come so softly that the guineas were not aroused, and thus Andy, at work in his field of hay, did not know that she came to the farm. She came into Philly's parlor fanning her face with her old hat, a tall, strong girl of twenty-four, strengthened and made gentle by much hard work.

"I walked over from the store after Brother Joe took me that way with the bucket of cream. I've got to get back in time to milk three cows against Pap and the boys quit work. Walk back, I will, but I said to Brother Joe he could let me out and I'd stop to see Cousin Philly." She was a pleasant girl, laughing a great deal. She laughed at stories she had to tell of the cows, of the work, of the boys, and she laughed again when she told about the hens that had stolen nests under a thorn bush.

"And there they are, three. As if they'd know I couldn't put my hand in there and catch a single one out. . . ." Her moist face shone in the dim light of Philly's room, and she rocked brightly to and fro, having a holiday out of the old rocking-chair, out of her short free afternoon.

"See Giles Wilson today?" Philly asked.

"Go on, Cousin Philly," Imogene said, beginning to laugh again.

"I bet you see Giles afore you go much further. Whyn't you marry Giles? Run off from your pap and do what you're a mind to. Let your old pap, old man Cundy, marry again and bring a woman there. Iffen you run off he'll find somebody right off, you'll see. He's too easy-goen to stir out and find himself a wife. There's a plenty would jump at the chance, good hard-worken women too."

Imogene laughed at this idea, but when she stopped her laughter Philly saw that there were tears in her eyes. She laughed again and this made a channel for the water of her eyes, for a large tear was running now over her indented cheeks. She dried her face with her skirt and she said that her father would not let Giles Wilson come on the place and that she would never see Giles any more, she supposed.

"He owns a farm. What's to hinder?" Philly talked fast then and repeated her admonitions. "You do like I say. As well work in Giles Wilson's kitchen as in old man Sam Cundy's and better. Giles, he's close, but he's thrifty, and a man is bound to be close in these hard times. You run off and marry Giles Wilson and I'll give you a wedden with oysters from town, and invite everybody you're a mind to. Candy and oranges. I'm your mother's own cousin. What's to hinder?"

There was an argument, both speaking at one time. Then Philly felt the need to whisper come over her. She swept her chair near to Imogene's and she leaned forward and said:

"Iffen you don't take Giles Wilson now Effie Trigg, she'll have him. She's ripe to catch. And Giles, he's as easy caught a man as ever is."

Imogene listened to Philly's whispering, her eyes opened wide, her face white, and she was confused between surprise and anger. Philly was whispering again.

"When a man acts the way Giles does it's a sign he's got you in head, but in head or out, when a fat girl like Effie is around, she gets past a man's

head. She laughs all over her fat. Her whole raw
meat laughs in a man's face. I'm here to tell you all
I know. . . ."

She sat back suddenly, pushing back her chair,
and she made as if no whispering had been. She
began to talk about the wedding she would provide, of the food and the invited guests. Imogene
laughed again, her plump white face and moist
hands deeply agitated. "Oh, Cousin Philly," she
said. She could not see how Philly could afford a
wedding for her. Philly needed a dress, she said.
Where would all the money come from? It would
cost twenty dollars, or perhaps more. She laughed
more faintly at the thought of twenty dollars spent
on foolishness and gave up the wedding as impossible.

"You run off with your clothes some day next
week and you just leave the rest to me," Philly
said. "There's a plenty in the way of money. I
always favored you above all my cousins and I'm
a mind to see you settled in life. One day the last
of next week."

"Iffen the cream happens to turn that day I
couldn't come," Imogene said. "I never can tell,
looks like, what day the cream will turn."

"Let the cream turn," Philly said. "There'll be
cream to turn at Giles Wilson's. Let it turn."

Philly made plans swiftly. She promised a wedding with oysters and cake, a lavish promise.

"Giles Wilson, when he stops by our house, we don't talk about to marry. It's little he ever says nohow," Imogene said.

"He means marry, no matter what he talks. I know by the look on a man. What does he talk about?"

"He'll say his house needs paint, maybe, or he'll say the kitchen chimney smoked today and he'll ask me what do I reckon caused it."

"Have you ever been inside his house?"

"I never was there, no."

"It's a bachelor's house, little inside it. I'll tell you what-all's inside it in case you want to know."

Imogene blushed at this, but she laughed too, and Philly knew that she wanted to hear all that she had to tell, that her mind would dwell on each named object and remember each exactly. Placing Giles among the things and moving him here and there before them, she would touch him anew when her mind made the pictures, and she would remember each thing described and know how each was set.

"Well, firstplace, you go in the front door off the porch where the hound dogs, three maybe, are as like as not asleep. The hall is wide but not very

long, square almost. By the front door, to prop
the door open in summer, is the old dinner horn
Giles's grand-mammy used to call home the men to
dinner with, and on a peg beside the parlor door
is the fox horn, a long horn almost the length of
my arm, and this Giles uses when he goes out to
hunt foxes moonlight nights in the fall. That's
all there is in the hall, every blessed stick.

"Then the parlor, on the right. You go inside
the door and there's not one blessed stick of furniture or thread or rag of carpet. Bare it is. Dust on
the floor. Ready for some wife to come in and fix
it up whatever way she pleases. Across the hall on
the left hand is Giles's room. You go inside the
door and on the right is a little table with a lamp
on it and some papers. Then along the wall you
come to a chair and on it is Giles's Sunday clothes
he bought last year. Then you come to the bed-
stead. Walnut, it is, and on it is a feather bed
Giles got when his mammy died, and I helped
Susan Wilson pluck the feathers for it. The dark
quilt Susan quilted with her own hand is folded
up over the place where the pillows are, but you
can't see whe'r they are white or colored because
the quilt hides what they are. Then next along
the other wall comes a chest and over it hangs a
little, small mirror with a squint in it. It's here

Giles combs his hair. Against the far wall is the fireplace and on the mantel is a box where Giles keeps his screws and nails and whatnot. Beside the mantel is a cubbyhole, but I couldn't tell you what might be inside. That's all there is to the room besides three chairs, one with a soft bottom. Then there's the back room where Giles eats his dinner, and behind that the kitchen where the black woman that lives out on the farm cooks his victuals unless she can't come, and then Giles, he cooks for his own self. And at ne'er a window is one sign of a curtain, but I doubt iffen Giles ever knows they're lacken. It's a fine prospect for a woman. What now does he talk about? Say and tell me. I'm your mother's own cousin."

"Oh, he sits still in his chair for a spell and by and by he'll say three bad crop years, hand-runnen, it's as much as a man can stand. Then he'll say the corn looks pretty this week and wasn't that a fine rain we had yesterday? Or he'll say he's two thousand dollars in debt on the place, but, come a good crop year and he'll be able to pay off five hundred dollars. Says then he'll be only fifteen hundred in debt. He'll say that in whispers."

"When a man says a thing like that he means all he says and more." Philly nodded her head quickly, up and down, to convince Imogene, but it seemed to her then that her words were idle and foolish and that Imogene knew as much as she. "When a man talks to a woman about how much he owes it's a good sign," she said, trying to think of some better thing to say. "It's a sign he's got a good woman in his head. Nowadays a man has got to go in debt to own land and get on in the world. You run off with your clothes, like I said, one day last part of next week, and come here. Oysters from town, I'll have, and oranges."

"I don't know what you mean. A plenty of money? I never yet knew you, Cousin Philly, to tell what wasn't gospel." Imogene was puzzled out of all laughter. She rocked softly to and fro in the few minutes left of her holiday.

"I can't tell you how it'll be, but it'll happen." Philly wanted to make all secure before Imogene left. "You trust all to me. A dress, iffen you haven't got what you need. Maybe I sold my little bull calf to Mabley and Grimes for a big price. Maybe my hens are in a fine way, fifty eggs a day."

Imogene went away, laughing now, but confused and distrustful of what she heard. Philly watched her from the door and waved to her when she turned back once before she entered the highroad. At the mouth of the lane she was met by Giles Wilson and they went outward together.

When she was gone the excitement of her lingered about Philly all through the evening. Her danger, her quietness, her cool, shy passion, her uncertain laughter, her lover—these made a richness about her. Her dark hair was curly and she wore a part through one side of it, a white line through the dark crinkled mat that folded over her head, like a cap. Her father expected her to stay in his house. She was strong for a girl, doing the work of a seasoned housekeeper. There were days when she scarcely found time to comb the tight curl out of her hair and make the fine white part at the side of it. She would walk a little way with Giles when he met her on a road, and say good-bye to him at the curve of the road long before she came within sight of her home, and in her good-bye she would know how the house where he lived was set inside, placing him there in her last shy caress. She would beg him not to come to her home and she would walk later along the road, weeping.

Philly visited three houses, inviting people to come to the party, and on the highroad she asked several that she met. "I have invited enough," she said as she passed homeward after a visit to the hamlet, having visited the store and invited all that she met there. "I'll not invite e'er other person," she said, and she remembered a woman's voice saying, "Mr. Blair invited me." She thought happily of Mr. Blair, giving him respect in her mind, giving him obedience. It would have seemed a strange thing for Andy to invite any to a party. She had spoken of him with praise at the store when a woman said, "I expect old Andy will be right put out when he knows a party will be at his house. A man-person hasn't hardly got time for parties, seems, and all the expense and wear on your things." This speech had provoked Mr. Blair again to a fine myth and thence to a fine reality. "Mr. Blair is different from most," Philly said. "He never was a hand to blame me iffen I take it in head to have a party, or anything else I might have a fancy for."

Walking homeward she overtook four women who stood together at the place where the lane met the highroad. They were talking slowly, looking at each other, two looking together when they had finished some spoken opinion, as if they asked one another for advice. They leaned together, half whispering, but now and then one cried out sharply when she was moved to state her mind with clearness and firmness. Philly thought that they would be talking of her secret and of her party, but when she had stood listening she found that they were speaking of Imogene and of Mr. Cundy's hard demands. Two of them were angry, but another was fault-finding and full of complaint. The fourth was quiet and sad, listening to the rest. For a time, then, Imogene's state arose as being more of importance than the kettle of money, and Philly, holding the kettle high in her thought, found Imogene's plight here a more sad matter than formerly, as being sufficient in sadness to thrust the kettle aside. She looked quickly from one speaker to another, her eyes darting here and there. Eliza White stood opposite Philly, and while the women were talking, Philly saw that her eyes floated in a gathering moisture that made them seem large and full. Philly watched her eyes to see what kind of tears would flow when the water fell, and she remembered Imogene's large tear and wondered if these would be large too because they were brought out by the thought of Imogene's sad case. While this moisture gathered, the woman looked toward Ronnie Rudds as if more had been said earlier, as if some memory of another, one dead perhaps, had been called forth, and Emma Trigg said:

"I always let Effie Trigg have her beauty sleep

out. It's not right to call a young girl before she's ready to wake."

"Imogene up before day to make a breakfast for all those men. Gets them out into the field by late sunup."

"For a young girl she sees too hard a time."

The water overflowed from the eye and ran in a thin stream toward the cheek, making no globule. It stopped in its path and turned toward the nose, running weakly across the weary flesh, and the eyes, left unguarded and unmagnified, seemed spent and ineffectual now that their grief was gone. "Lispy Cundy said to me," the woman began, re-telling something she had told before Philly came, naming Imogene's mother and some request she had made. The moisture gathered at last to a small round tear and fell, leaving her face dry, and she stood by in apathetic inattention, unable now to weep or to give more, having given all that she had.

"For a young girl she sees too hard a time," another woman said, repeating.

"Sam Cundy acts the way you'd think he didn't have ten acres."

"It's trashy, I always think, to work so hard and never enjoy. It's like some other kind of people, not our kind."

"He acts so you'd think he came from away off, from up north where it's cold ten months or longer."

"You'd think he didn't come from around here, to see how he's always out to get more. In a fine shape, he is, hardly any debt, and what does he do but buy more land?"

"If Giles Wilson had any spunk he'd go in there some day and ride off with Imogene, and carry her to the county Judge or to some preacher."

"Giles has got a right smart of spunk now. I wouldn't be too quick to say a hard thing about Giles."

"Why won't he brace up then and take what's rightly his? Why won't he take Imogene's part?"

"Give Giles time, I say."

"Sam Cundy has been in a hard way since Tuesday 'twas a week ago. Giles has had time to stir."

"Since three weeks back and longer. He's been in a hard way of a kind since two months back. Hardly could you live in the house where he is."

"Cundy says he'll shoot Giles if he ever comes there again. Says he's got a shotgun loaded, and I wouldn't wonder he has."

"Sam talks loud, but I wouldn't hardly expect him to be free with a gun."

"The kind that talks loud and boasts in anger,

that's the kind that shoots easiest, I always noticed. I wouldn't put it far past Sam Cundy to shoot when he gets warmed up in anger."

"A group of us might go there, wait on old Sam as a committee, you might say, and put it up to him to let Imogene off to marry."

"Iffen Giles has got the spunk a man ought to have there won't be any call for e'er committee or the like."

"But I wouldn't put it far past Cundy to shoot, against his dander is aroused. He's that turn now since he's old. Wants all his own way and holds a belief that all his youngones belong fast to him forever. He'd make a mighty stir and maybe shoot to hurt somebody."

"Best wait a little. Wait. Giles might find a way for his own self."

"I've got it in mind to help Imogene," Philly said, having heard all this without speaking, looking quickly from one speaker to another. "I've got a scheme in my head. Just wait a little. I've had Imogene in mind all week and I'm not of a mind to leave her be much longer."

"We better go speak to Sam Cundy, I think," Ronnie Rudds said, having proposed this before. "Quiet him down before he has time to get heated up. Put the idea into his head right."

"We better wait now till after oat harvest maybe."

"After wheat harvest is long enough to wait," Philly called out, moving away. They were scattering apart, going homeward.

"Things will look different after harvest."

Leaving these women, Philly walked homeward along the lane. The kettle of bright money in the cubbyhole of the loft arose before her as a bright blossom coming to flower anew each instant. Her heart leaped in its beat for joy, and a joy at foretelling the praise and envy of the people when they knew of the good fortune quickened her steps. She was avid for more joy, for more praise, for more envy. Mr. Blair sat in the house during her absence, his eyes on the small door that guarded their money hoard. Seen thus, while she walked along the lane, he was a fine man, halfway a stranger, whom she had not married, whom she might marry, whom she scarcely knew at all. She had invited Callie Webster and Robbie May Rudds and she had told Callie to bring her children. She had invited Bonnie White and her grandfather, old Mr. Bonnie. She had heard Andy inviting Giles Wilson and she herself had sent a

message to Imogene. Coming through the gate
from the lane, she encountered Andy at the house
door speaking to someone who had come on an
errand, "And iffen you see Hez Turner tell him to
come."

"I thought you didn't favor to invite Hez?" she
said, as she came through the door.

"Let all come," he said with a great pride.
"Show favors to none. Iffen Hez Turner wants to
know my surprise I'm not a man to mistreat a
neighbor." It was a fine speech, coming from a
man who made a pleasant show as seen from outside, the pot being invisible but present and near.

"Preach and pray over the kettle, and maybe
convert somebody to his way," she said, "but no
matter."

A day passed over them, the hours winding
slowly around as they were marked by the clock
on the mantel. The kettle was brought out from
hiding and they looked into it to see that it was
secure. When they opened it to peer inside, Andy,
as if he acted secretly, took from it the little sack
containing the two pearls and he shut it into his
hand. Philly made no protest, and at that instant
it seemed to her that he claimed these two stones
as being more of his own than her own, as if he

had some greater right to a part of the treasure because he had first found it and had named it a kettle of gold before he had dug it from the earth. She was surprised that he should take out some part and retain it from their common keeping, but she said nothing, thinking that he would put the pearls back soon, and she closed the kettle and helped to set it away, knowing that he withheld the stones. But each time that she looked into the pot or stirred the coins about with her finger she knew that Andy still kept the little sack containing the pearls. On the third day after it left the pot she began to wonder what he had done with it, but she did not ask after it.

She made her house ready for a gathering of people, brushing the dust from the rooms. Andy seemed unable to hold his hands on the plow with any steadiness. He brought the beast he had been working back to the barn and he left the plow overturned at the edge of the cornfield. Later Philly saw him wandering up and down the farm without employment, and at noon he broke his food into bits which he left uneaten while he expressed distrust and displeasure. The people of the neighborhood were a gossipy set, he said, and not a truth-telling set either. He told a story which put a sinister character on Rudds, his neighbor.

He himself had seen a man hiding in the woods, and he had seen strange footmarks in the soft loam of the cow pen. After the noon meal he went above to the upper room and he found a more secure hiding-place for the kettle. He went back and forth on the stairs through the afternoon, his mind a tumult of bolts and keys.

He asked Philly to find the key that would fit the little brass lock. She emptied the spools and buttons from a basket and turned out table drawers that had caught the drift from many years of living. She searched into an old teapot and she picked over screws and buttons and little broken ends of things long out of use, looking into all the small corners of the house. While she looked for the key she looked as well for the small sack containing the two pearls, being secret of this however, but she could find it nowhere in the house. She began to wonder why Andy had taken it from the kettle and why he had hidden it away from her, and as time passed she was amused and pleased that he should have a secret. She was not displeased that he should have the pearls for himself alone, for, since he had first called the hidden thing under the stump a pot of gold, he was entitled to something more of it than she could claim.

Searching, she went up into the garret of the house, beyond the upper room, and she felt into an old wooden box that was hidden among the logs of the rafters, and her hand touched old square-shafted nails and a few wooden pins that had been trimmed for some forgotten purpose. She turned old letters out of a tea caddy and knew that these missives had come from her sister Susie a long while since and that at some time she would read them again, but now she must find the key that would fit the small brass lock. She pulled out a little secret drawer that was hidden back in the cubbyhole by the fireplace, that made there a profound secrecy where a few worthless things had been put away and forgotten, her hand fumbling in the dark among little garden seeds and taps and trinkets.

She fitted keys into little slits and tried to make them turn bolts over, and she went again to look into the smallest and most secret place of the house, the secret drawer in the dark cubbyhole, remembering then that Susie had six children and if she had lost there would be six to help her find. She was weary and warm from the search, having been up and down stairs and ladders, bending and searching and feeling, and she thought here of Andy as having been too stingy to give her any children, as having held back a part of what he should have given her, as taking what he wanted and holding back some little final thing. She leaned into the dark of the cubbyhole, into the odors of mice and moths and wood borers, dust and lint and vague mold, looking meanly down into the last crevice to satisfy Andy, to find for him, thinking thus of him as she fumbled in the dark.

The deep gray twilight of the cubbyhole was darkened by her own shadow, for she had crawled into the small doorway. Her fingers fumbled among old spider webs that had become heavy with dust and age. She reached into dust and mold and her fingers took meanings and minute forms from the bits that she fumbled, the ends of herself meeting the fine ends of these withered things and bringing a picture of what they would appear to be if they were seen, so that she smelt the feel of them and felt the smell of them, crawling into the blackness. Thus her double search, for a key and a sack, became a triple search in which she probed Andy minutely to see where he lacked.

The shadows of the trees began to lengthen and the summer evening gathered, the evening of the party having come. Andy milked the cow early, scarcely waiting for the sunlight to pass from the house wall. Philly threw the hens a hasty supper of corn. Fear had replaced Andy's delight in his treasure, and as he milked the cow his head was lifted now and then to watch the lane that came toward the house. He scarcely drew his share of the milk, yielding to the calf in his distress. He passed Philly in his hurry to regain the house and he said to her:

"I saw fresh footprints behind the barn. It's my belief, Philly, this house; it's watched. That's my belief."

"Watched how?" Philly asked.

"It comes to my mind we'd better not show the kettle of money tonight. We can name what the surprise is but we better not bring it out to show. I wouldn't trust all that gang that's to be here. I saw Lester Rudds outside awhile back and he says the whole Elk Creek country is a-comen here tonight, the white-trash, even."

"Is the cow dry you can't get more'n a pint outen her? What manner or way is that to treat a cow?" Philly saw unpleasantness gathering about the party, and being unwilling to yield her antici- pated pleasure she complained for the lack of the milk. "I wouldn't trust you to milk my cow again.

. . . I wouldn't trust that-there gang that's to be here, neither," she added after a little.

"It comes to my mind we'd best not show the kettle," Andy said again, coming to the kitchen on tiptoes. "We'd best hide it deeper and not let e'er one see."

"Well, you better hide quick if you expect, Andy, to find a safe place before they come. Callie always was a before-hand person and she'll be here soon now."

Her thought leaped outward toward the rolling tilt of the land beyond the house where she stood and beyond the barn lot and the pasture, beyond the cornfield that reached north and west. Eastward before the front of the house the lane reached outward toward the highroad, and a little way beyond stood the small house, painted white, where Hester Trigg lived. South, and the road wound down to the village. Back again along the way, the village left behind, past Bonnie's and Hester Trigg's and past the lane, and the road then swept outward to Stoner's white house and his hay field, but a little beyond it wound downward between the bluffs to cross the creek and mount upward again, sweeping then outward toward the west, going far, the old graveyard back on the hill to the left, and farther came Giles

Wilson's. The land tipped and tilted, cornfields and tobacco just beginning to get a stand, the wheat yellow and near the harvest, the oats high and green. Darting about, outward, the land became a changing and widespread vagueness that tilted in large masses and rolled outward into vague darkness beyond the reach of the twilight and the moon. The extended reach of it, peopled and farmed, pressed inward upon themselves, herself and Andy, while she stood at the door of the house in the early twilight and listened to the hot-weather locusts crying in the grass and the frogs in the wet place in Bonnie's pasture.

"Oh, what made us invite all that riff-raff here?" Andy cried out. "No place inside the house will be safe once it's known there's a kettle of money. Roam all over the house, they will, and find anything you might have put by."

He listened, turning his ear toward the lane, as if he might hear the tramp of people coming. He looked to Philly for assistance and he cursed his bad luck, blaming her for the party which was at hand. "I'm a mind to take the kettle and run off and hide myself, but it's a heavy load to carry."

"We could bury it," Philly said. "We could bury it somewhere until morning."

"Yes, we could bury it, but where? I wouldn't

trust the spot it was buried in to be out of my sight, not with the whole of that gang on the place. Talk quick and tell me where we could bury it."

"Oh, we could bury it under the floor. Under the house then." She named five or six places. "Oh, we could bury it under the hearthstone." The whole outside was spreading farther, gathering force, to press inwardly upon her. "Under the stone," she said.

Andy went quickly to get his ax and his spade. He worked quickly, biting at his cheeks in his misery of mind, stopping to listen to the tramp of feet he could hear coming over the hills and over the distant roadways. He pried up a large gray stone of the hearth, using his pick, and he laid the stone aside on the floor, finding it heavy to lift. Then he dug into the hard-pounded clay that lay beneath, earth that had never before been disturbed, and Philly brought a basket to take away the clay which was lifted from the place. When he had made a hole of the size he had well in mind they went above-stairs and brought the treasure vessel and set it securely into the hole and they covered it over with a napkin. Philly lifted the iron lid to look once inside the pot before she dropped the napkin to place for the last time, and she knew, secretly, without comment, that the pearls were not there.

When Andy had lifted back the stone he made it fit into place as if it had never been lifted, but it was not so tight as formerly, being cradled now in new-laid soil. He carried the basket of unused clay to the garden and emptied it there, and as he returned he called to Philly to hurry, saying that he heard steps now surely.

"Hearken to me," he said, half in threat, his finger lifted in her face. "Ne'er a word is to be said that the surprise is a kettle of money. You hear? Say not a word about the pot. Ne'er a word."

"What will we name for the surprise?" she asked. Her eyes were blinking as if they went in and out before her face. A large up-and-down motion jerked forward and back, about to strike her shoulder, and Andy's hand sawed the air just above her throat. "We have got to have a surprise, now we've promised one. What surprise will we name?" She shrank from the question even while her own voice was asking it, but she thrust it forward over and over. "What surprise? What?" she asked.

"Ne'er a word about the money," he said. "You hear what I say."

She was hushed into obedience, feeling a hard

and determined force behind the finger that beat the air just beyond her face. "Mr. Blair ever was a strong-minded man," she whispered, speaking to the storeman off at the town to the north. She went to the kitchen dresser where she thrust the comb hurriedly through her hair to make ready for the company. Knotting her hair, she saw through the dim window a young man waiting in the field just beyond the fence, keeping apart among the bushes. She had never seen this strange person before, but she remembered what Andy had said of strange footmarks about the barn. A curious man was walking about under the trees outside and a pot of money was hidden under the hearthstone. She could scarcely add these facts together to make them yield a sum. She stumbled up the stairs and she put on her best dress quickly, whispering to herself. The whole countryside was coming to view their surprise and they had none to reveal. She longed momentarily for the old-time unconsciousness and ease, for the day when a hidden pot of money had never come into her thought.

"I hear steps, Mr. Blair," she called out, coming below, the nearness of the guests already shaping her thought to a new strangeness. She was fastening her dress at the throat. There were many voices at the door.

II

THE HOT-WEATHER BEETLES CRIED ALL DAY, MAKING a clicking sound that burst out of the weeds and the grass, out of the half-grown corn and the thick tufts of the wheat. The grain fields turned about with the turning of the land, arising and dipping past the limits of the wire fences, rolling up into the washed-out places where a few locust trees held the land together and made a faintly darkened line against the brightening wheat. The land rolled forward toward the harvest, or it rolled backward toward the time of planting, toward the long sequence of harvests and plantings, moving backward, over and over, the soil turning, revolving under the plowings of many springs. Back further toward the trees and the uncleared forests, or forward swiftly to the acute moment, the fine and most immediate present, where a man draws a reaping machine out of a barn, oiling the parts, saying, "In three days, or a week at the longest, we'll begin to cut, if the signs hold good."

The streams wound through the land, having cut deep channels as they had been flowing many centuries through the limestone. One stream flowed north between darkened bluffs that cut the turfland and the plowed fields apart, but it curved westward and turned then to flow south, mile after mile, crossed by narrow roads that ran over bridges—iron webs between two high bluffs. There were small houses and large ones, mostly painted white, set wide in the sun or shaded by old trees, and these were the living-places of the men who were tilling the fields and preparing the harvest. The men were dispersed to the fields, but at the burying-place they were gathered together, their names written on stone—Wilson, Blair, Rudds, Bonnie, Trigg, Roundtree, Turner, Shepherd, and others, written there on the faces of rocks.

Ben Shepherd, a boy seventeen, crossed these, the upper waters of Pigeon River, and walked about through the hilly rises. Intent on going forward, intoxicated with motion and fatigue, he had dismissed from his mind much that he knew of the world by the way of his own lived past, and as he stepped, choosing his way at the side of the rough road, he viewed with pride the fine void he had brought to his memory. A man who had given him a ride had called him a "hitch-hiker." He had wanted to become nothing so that he might then try a new way of being. The road wound over a hilly country amid a dense wayside growth. He followed the droop of the land as it sank and rose with the turnings of the creek, and now and then the vague and continual query that haunted his mind would take the form of some stated question, as, "Where does color go when it fades from the sky?" As, "Where?" or "Why?" or "How is it thus?" As if the land had in him become conscious, as if it would ask these things.

He had eaten an abundant breakfast at a farmhouse far back along the way, and still replete, wanting nothing, he thought that he would leave the road and fare for the day on the scant lunch he had bought at a country store. Back of these contrivings flowed a ghost of old clauses that fell flatly and unattended in his mind, thus: "The cavalry did not dare to begin to cross (make a beginning of crossing). . . . A friendship that brings slavery on the state must not be sought by

us. . . . Publius Sextius has been weakened by
wounds so severe that he cannot hold himself
up. . . . Ut rebus conlocandis tempus daretur
. . . so that there was no time for arranging
things. . . ."

The land spread out in great masses when he
walked on a ridge, but he sank down into the folds
of it when he dropped from the ridge to the turning creek channel. From the highest hills he could
see the line of Knobs to the south, and they were
blue along the horizon in a long, broken chain, as
if they would be mountains. Lying about, beyond
his sight now, but realized, were the more level
farms that rolled away through the central Ken-
tucky plain, and these would be planted or left in
pasture. Close at hand the rugged bluffs and
turned stones had been washed by the rains and
snarled by lightning. The earth itself, Terra—the
first, the earliest, the most ancient oracle, the most
profound deity—showed herself here in the be-
ginnings of lesser mountains and little rivers. Ben
climbed among tangled hills and walked all morning along a broken roadway that overlooked rough
glades.

A woman took him into an old car among bags
of feathers and wool. She was going to the store to
trade, she said, and he left her where the road

crossed Elk Creek, taking the way down the
stream. He thought that this would be the land
over which Harrod had hunted when the first set-
tlers had lived in the forts; Harrod, the founder
of Harrod's Fort, had doubtless walked over these
actual hills, a tall man of great bulk, hunting to
supply the people within the walls when there was
danger from the Indians that came down from
Ohio to get the scalps of the white men. Men of
his own breed, fathers of his fathers' fathers, had
been there. He knew very little about them beyond the names. Tobias Shepherd, the father of
John, who was the father of Joel, the father of
John B.—thence Richard, John F. and themselves
—all. Tobias had been with Harrod. He continually thought that Tobias Shepherd had hunted
with Harrod here among the jagged bluffs and
rolling woodlands, and thinking this, he wanted
the land to be of a more undivided and uncharted
sort and he rejected the fences and the water-
gaps as if he would gently push each one out of
sight and ignore it thereafter. They, those men,
were mythical giants stalking through the land in
long leathern shirts and breech-garments that
scarcely covered the knees. They had cleared the
soil of the trees, a little at a time, generation after
generation getting itself born for the labor.

A faintly sung poetry of words following words knocked lightly at his memory, a measure of much that he knew of the world as he had lived it, thus:

> hortor
> hortaris
> hortatur
> hortamur
> hortamini
> hortantur

The stream lay outspread now through the deep valley, winding among sycamores and willows, with a few old beeches showing their gray trunks farther in the rising glade. A fresh reminder of Harrod appeared in his thought with a sudden up-swelling of admiration and good feeling, and he wondered then if people always loved their ancestors and made them famous for whatever they had done. He liked better to dwell on the giants that had manned the forts, fought the aborigines out of the land, cut out the forests, and turned the rolling land into fenced farms. He saw them going forward with whatever they had contrived, their guns in their hands. He wanted to ask somebody if this were actually the land over which the men from Harrod's must have hunted. He answered the query to his own liking, wanting it to be the same. "Ut rebus conlocandis" blew again

over his thought as a spent wind. He had learned
this phrase too well; it would not entirely depart.
No path lay under his feet. The houses of the
farms stood remotely placed, one on this distant
rise and one on another, all back on the rolling
land beyond the creek that flowed through a
ravine. He crossed and recrossed the stream, walking through the tangled growth or on the stones
of the shallow water.

He came to a ledge that stood out as a shelf from
the wall of stone. Thinking that the ledge would
shelter one from rain he stopped there. A faint
knowledge of this place came to his mind, as if
some former memory of it were at hand, as if he
had never been there before and yet remembered
it. The place and the singing verb were mingled.
It was such a place as Harrod might have chosen
for shelter. "Hortor hortaris," was the vaguely satisfying answer, and some whisper said, "It is indeed such a place."

There were flat stones now underfoot. He
looked at the creek in the channel below him, the
green-banked wall on the opposite side, the corn
in the high field above. He had eased himself of
his burden. From some distant place he heard the
slow lilting of a farm bell, and then another in a
remote and unrelated key. The country seemed

dissevered, the parts unrelated, the high thin quality of the last bell having no relation to the flat metallic gonging of the first, having none with the deeply rutted creek, none with the woman off at the low hamlet trading her wool and her feathers. He decided to stay here. When he had rested he searched about for a spring in the ledge and he soon found one. He hid his things under the brush and walked to the hamlet, the afternoon now being well gone. Whatever traders had visited the store during the afternoon were gone now, and the shop was quiet in the afternoon sunlight. He bought supplies for himself and carried them back to his rocky shelter where he lit a fire and cooked a supper of bread and fresh meat.

During the night rain fell and at morning the water of the creek ran tawny. Seeing ripe berries floating on the brink, Ben went up the stream to find the berry bushes.

Having chosen a ledge as a place for shelter he had a sense of the entire reach of the country, one part as fitting as another and no part binding him entirely to one valley or one hill. He would stay there in the half-grot, but he had no obligation to it, and no sense of need, as if he might at

any moment be up the stream or down, or out on
the fields or pastures, dwelling anywhere, or everywhere. The rim of the east hill lay along the horizon in rolling lumps of slightly heaving masses, a
great god lain down to sleep at the edge of the
sky. To the north another mass turned in a loose
design and came to rest toward the northwest
point. There would be an old graveyard somewhere about, and there the graves of the Shepherds—Tobias, John, Joel, John B., Richard, and
others—would lie crookedly about as these names
had been put crookedly into the earth; for they
were dry, withered names of ancient men, were
words fading out ot an old Bible yeai after year ao
the inks decayed. All the people of this region
were of the Shepherds, by close links or distant
marryings. He had come to get the names off the
tombstones. Going up the stream, looking for the
berries, he felt a deep and near relation to the
graveyard as if he belonged there more than to
any other place in the whole countryside, and he
thought that he would be working among the
tombs before the end of the day.

The briars were not difficult to discover. Some
of the ripened berries had been pelted to the
ground by the shower and these had already been
taken by the ants. While he gathered berries from

the bushes, some birds, in flocks, darted uneasily in the brush and the trees, making scolding noises, and the flock denied him the right there. He ate the berries until he was satisfied with them, and later he gathered more to carry away in his quart cup. He wondered if he might live in the country for a little while as Harrod had lived, getting his food directly from the beasts and the herbs. The abundance of the berries gave him a security beyond the hostility of the birds, as if in the fruits the whole land contrived to establish him in a way of life.

He walked through an old pasture among the uplands. Hidden in a tangled thicket he looked out on a farm where a tall man worked over a fence, the sound of the hammer, as it pounded the staples, coming amplified across the small hollow. Ben sat in the thicket to watch the work of the fence-builder. The morning was heavy and warm after the rain of the night, the sun beating heavily through the moist air. The man was slow over the fence, which gave him much trouble, the wires slipping from his hands. He set two posts and tamped the earth about another, going from one part of the labor to another, scarcely finishing anything.

Ben remembered a small field-glass and reaching into his pocket he found one and he adjusted this so that it gave him a view of the small objects on the opposite slope. In the glass the man was a wonder of patches and sewed-up kinds of cloth fitted neatly together, his bulging rheumatic knees being sewed into fitted pockets of cloth. As he worked the man praised himself continually as a skilled mender of fences. Broken phrases of this comment came flatly across the hill with the knock of the hammer, both followed by a faint echo. There were pleased comments upon the work of the hammer, but a curse went after the tool if any part of the fencing went wrong. Then a woman came to move about near the man, and a dog lay on the ground not far away, coming uncertainly into the small glass as if it had been there all the while.

"Go to the devil!" a hard voice called, coming out of the hot earth where the brow of the pasture hill lay bare in the sun. The man had held the hammer out in his hand and looked at it, the act accompanying the words the hill had spoken. They stood in the bright hot air, the man drawing again at the wires, the woman standing by to make comment. She folded her arms under her apron to guard them from the heat of the sun. She walked about with short, uneven steps, darting here and there.

"I reckon you're not a hungry man," she spoke out, her words beating sharply out of the hill.

Ben thought that he would go, that he would find some bait and fish in the stream, but he stayed to watch the two actors, fastened to his place by their senseless movements. The woman was small and quick, impatient of the patched man, but he worked at the wires until he had worn her to apathetic submission. Then he went over the fence into a cornfield and he began to hack at an old stump, making firewood. The dog, a great brown hound, went back and forth from the man to the woman, and when she began to gather the wood in her apron the dog lay on the ground, but it leaped suddenly to the stump and barked, clawing at the disturbed earth. The woman called the man Andy, and knowing by what name the man would be called, Ben settled the name upon him and listened carefully to hear some name by which to know the woman.

"What's taken the dog?" Andy asked. "I never see the dog in such a swivet before."

The woman turned away, her apron full of the cut wood. The dog was beautiful, leaping about the stump, making quick arcs through the air, crouching and springing over the torn earth of the cornfield, trampling the corn. He barked a wild, quick, short laughter, imploring the man, imploring the ax.

Ben climbed a small oak, merged with the dark gray and brown of the trunk, his clothes being brown. He clung to the trunk, catching at snarled boughs and coming finally to a higher place where he settled himself to a crotch, keeping behind foliage and limbs. When he was fixed there he could see the wreckage of the stump and, with his glass, he could see the parted earth. The man now seemed disconnected with the earth before which he moved, his ax sharply divided from the horizon against which it leaped, himself out of partnership with the brown soil and the short green corn, as if he were enacting some part of an imagined piece. "It's a pot of gold!" his voice was crying out, a loud cracked phrase that seemed to come out of the hill. "It's a pot, I say. Gold! What else?"

The man lashed great strokes into the broken stump. By the time that Ben had made himself secure in the tree, Andy had torn the stump well apart, half fighting now with the dog. His distressed cries mingled with his oaths and with the bark of the dog and were the one point at which he touched the earth. Then the words came clear again, sharply cut before the hill, and he paused an instant.

"It's a pot of gold!" The phrase leaped forward, each word shaded by a faint echo. The crisp words lay then in a said phrase and the ax leaped into its business again. Without ceasing to dig, the man called out again and again, "Philly, a pot of money. Gold! A pot, I say. . . ."

The woman came back, holding the wood in her apron, her words, "Plow-iron . . . broken plow . . ." coming in a flat stratum of sound across the hill. Andy cuffed the dog and pushed it aside, and the two actors in the scene, Andy and the woman he called Philly, leaned together over the dug place, both pulling at some object that lay under the ground, their bodies bent and their strength set against the earth. The woman laughed and withdrew from the act, laughing at the man, but presently she leaned over the task again. Ben looked away from the two, and back again. They continued to draw their arms about and voices spoke for them, saying, "Gold . . . pot . . ." Ben wanted to shout, to raise a great halloo, to bring back the accustomed ways of life to the hillside, a vast halloo that would open the hills and startle the fields and creeks, that would break the land apart and unite it again in its accustomed harmony of part unlike part in a familiar piece.

He was about to begin a great noise when the

two on the hillside became very still, both leaning together. Ben thought of figures—"gleaners"; and here they thought that they were gleaning gold. The earth yielded under their force and some object came from the ground, pulled forward by their gleaning hands. They were hovering over the matter as ants over a sweet sop, and they talked together, making quick signs and breaking away the clay with their hands. He saw the object over which they were bent. Their hands were large over a vessel and their fingers moved with the ax. The lid was taken from the pot and their astonishment and fear mingled a moment and stood to the fore, annihilating their pleasure.

The woman, Philly, wept and beat her hands together and talked, but her words were lost in passing across the hollow. She walked apart from the vessel, making signs with her hands. They carried the object over the fence and the man covered it with the apron, but the apron blew aside once and Ben saw money in the vessel. The man was crying and beating his hands, and the woman looked fearfully about as if she suspected some watcher of the scene. The man took up the ax and dug into the hole, searching for more, but nothing further was found. The dog was indifferent now, having wandered away.

Andy and Philly went, taking their pot of gold or whatever coin they had found. They carried it to the fence and lifted it over into the pasture.

They were gone soon after, the two of them carrying the pot between them, staggering under the heavy load. They would set it down now and then and face each other, talking, making gestures, laughing together. At last they sank into the low-lying droop of the pasture and went beyond the vision of the oak. A house, stained brown by the weather, arose out of the curve of the hill down the way they had gone.

Ben fished in the stream all the afternoon, smiling whenever he thought of the kettle of money and of the two drab bodies bending over it to draw it from the earth. The secrecy of the pot was a seductive thought that came to him continually, lying under every other recognition, so that it made a shape that entered into his dreams when he slept under the ledge. On the following day he was still under the spell of the kettle. He walked among the fields and pastures, viewing impartially all that he met there, keeping himself apart. He went near the house into which the kettle had been taken and he watched there for a time, but he could see no sign of recent good fortune upon the house. Late in the day, while he waited for the merchant to wrap his package, he came near to speaking of the pot. He looked at the man's yellow mustache and his half-closed eyelids, the eyes bent on the yellow paper he was folding about the parcel, and he caught his breath inward to say, "Hear about the kettle of gold found over in Blair's cornfield?"; but a quiet seemed to press inward upon his throat, to push the words gently back, and when the man looked up suddenly, Ben asked another thing.

"Do you know the place where the old family named Shepherd used to bury?"

The man told him, giving careful directions for finding the spot. It would be a mile toward the north, beyond the creek, his finger pointing vaguely behind, his thumb thrown upward. "They were among the first to come here," he said, "or so I was always told. And all now gone off or buried, till there's not a man's son alive of that name in the whole district. . . ."

"Tobias Shepherd was the first," Ben said. "He was one of Harrod's men. I'm the seventh generation from Tobias. . . ."

Ben knew that he was boasting and he half
feared to hear the man reply, "Very well, take the
seventh chair." He left the store in the slanting
light of the late afternoon and he made a wide cir-
cuit, walking three miles, to try to find the place
where the Shepherds were buried. Toward dusk
he found a small, brush-grown plot of a half acre
or more, and all about in the undergrowth were,
standing or fallen, the stones that marked the
burying sites. The place seemed well filled, a stone
and another, dotting the green herbs and dimly
seen through the brush, and Ben, looking about,
discovering more and more of them, had a fine
pride that there were so many.

He lay down to sleep in his ledge shelter soon
after he had eaten, knowing that he would go to
the graveyard the next day, when the light would
be clear on the stones. He was weary and his eyes
were sick with the struggle they had made to read
the words that were cut into the rock. The richness of the burying-place in its multitude gave him
a new sense of the country as it spread here and
there beyond his ledge, as if the people and their
generations had become a florescence that arose
with branchy stems and wide flowerings that
reached into every hollow and spread up over
every hill, dividing again and again.

In the morning he found that the ants had got into the box where he kept his food and were crawling in a dense horde over his bacon. He had a great disgust of the insects and he knew suddenly that they were under all the soil, working in hurried aimlessness that somehow took purpose and order in the whole mass of them. He threw away the spoiled food and went to the village to buy more.

Late in the morning he came again to the Shepherd burying-place and rested from the heat seated beyond the fence under a drooping crab tree. The small graveyard reached in irregular curves and angles across a lightly sunken hilltop. The place was grown over with stunted crab trees and thorns, and a grapevine hung a long festoon from the top of an elm. The weather had plucked little identations unevenly over the stones so that the letters cut there were hard to decipher, for the carvings fainted away continually into the more mystical suggestions put there by the elements. Some crows were making soft, hoarse cries on a farther hill, and now and then the sound took on the quality of a murmured human speech that followed a low shrill outcry, all being subdued.

When he had looked at many of the stones, seeing that the letters and figures faded into the

marks of the weather, making out a name here
and a date there, he sat to rest again under the
crab tree. A sharp pricking on his hand that rested
on the ground, and he looked down to see that an
ant was running over his fingers. They had a keen
appetite for meat and for all meaty substances, he
reflected. They would have eaten all that was soft
underground. He hated them then, and he
knocked another from his fingers, calling out,
"You little devil!" He wondered if he might in
any way outwit them and if he might be able to
save his food from their spoliation. They were
everywhere, under every rood of the ground.
While he thought of the ants the low gurgled
sound, cries as of speech and laughter, continued,
as if some sound were coming from the graves, but
they were matted with grass and bushes and were
sunken to an evenness with the ground. Searching
into the undergrowth he found a gravestone on
which KITTY SHEPARD was rudely spelled. There
was a hardness and a resisting squareness in the
lettering on this stone, KITTY SHEPARD set with a
deep indentation along the front of the rock, and
the remembered phrase, "Groups of pyramids,
large and small, at Gizeh," set his verbal-noun
singing in mind, all related now to this unyielding
Kitty whose name was written "pard," as if cut or

outlined in the word itself were the two rude stony lions.

He worked through a tangled hedge, searching for more stones, coming now to the graves of the elders where no letterings had been left, where perhaps few had been attempted. Determined to go forward, pushed back, struggling, yielding at one place but thrust forward at another, he went more deeply into the glade. The whole object became the intention to push through the tangle of shrubs at the point he had attempted. He broke into violent sweat and tingled with the plucking thorns.

Suddenly there came a moment when the brush no longer resisted his forward-hurling body. He pressed through the low tangled boughs and came into a place where no shrubs were growing. The cleared space was roughly six or eight feet square, and overhead the boughs met in a matted roof. His flesh was on fire and he was angry that the briars had plucked him in many places. His flesh continued to tingle and snarl, as if flesh had no place here, as if the tearing thorns and hurt nerve-ends were at war.

It was cool here in this grot of boughs, and he sat on the ground to let the heat subside from his tingling flesh. In the center of the small tract there was a depression in the earth, a trough that was grown with a fine bluegrass such as is produced in rich shaded places. He rolled up his trousers and took away his socks to cool his legs and he searched the backs of his arms to see what scratches he had got from his struggle through the brush.

Then he saw that there were some white stones imbedded in the long bluegrass, within the shallow trough that lay in the middle of the cleared space. He wondered at the stones for a little, sucking at his plucked arm and wiping a trace of blood from his wrist. When he had satisfied his hurts he leaned over and began to turn the stones up into the light, and he saw that they were not stones, but the bones of a man. They were laid in no order, but were dragged about and discarded or rolled into a heap. A long thigh-bone lay crossed over an arm-piece. The little knuckles were scattered or rolled into a heap. Parts were missing. There was only one thigh. A part of the skull was gone. The animal matter was so leached away that these parts which were left were stony, were but shapes cast in whitened lime.

Ben took up these relics and looked at each one, or he fitted each one back into its grassy mat. The ants had left them, or if any ant ran over one she regarded it as if it were a stone, taking nothing from it. His mind would go, again and again, to all the parts that go into the making of man, to all the curious tubes and contrivances and juices that are put over or within these calcine emblems. These would be the bones of some ancient Shepherd, perhaps the first, the strongest, or of the one born in the fort, having had the whole of a man's strength. He measured the thigh-bone against his own, knowing that the fleshly body lacked the whole of its growth.

The bones seemed familiar then, and he wondered why men counted them as fearful objects. They went with a man wherever he went and their shapes were continually under his hand, to be felt and known. He lifted his own thigh, seeing how a thought might heave a bone forward or settle it back, upward or down. While he speculated thus of the bones, settling them back into their grassy places, he heard the low clatter of musical comment that ran continually through the glade with now and then a sound like a woman's voice speaking some light word of protest or daring, some laughter, as if the voices were speaking and replying in phrases of such a lilt as this:

"Nine, it's nine!"

"What will anybody do with it?"

"A murmur with nothing to fill it, with nothings and nothings to keep it. What is nine?"

All at once it seemed strange to him that there should be voices in the glade, although at first the sounds had been granted and passed as if they were of the same substance as the wind. He took one of the bones, a long foot-finger, a metatarsus, and he thrust it into his pocket. Then he rolled his trousers back over his legs and adjusted his socks, and he started back through the brush. The voice would cry out some high woman's speech, some word such as "Mine" or "Nine." For an instant he thought that the voice said "Mine," and that it claimed the bone he had taken, and he wanted to hurry away from the place before it spoke again.

The sounds seemed nearer as if they were coming closer. Tangled in the brush he had a terror of the sharp briars that held him with human fingers and laid long sharp claws into his skin. "It's mine!" a voice called out, a high sharp cry that sang through the glade. The briars plucked him back and the thorns worried his clothing and tore at his flesh. The snarls of the tight boughs twisted and bent together to make a fine net to hold him. He worked his shoulders into an opening and twisted to draw his body along the channel he had devised, but the boughs were unresisting. "It's nine!" the voice called flatly again, as if it meant to say "Mine!" He stopped, resting among the twisting twigs, and his feet were entirely off the ground. The thought that he had best fling away the bone he carried settled over his being, but an inner determined spark leaped up and took the form of a sharp spear of will that would not yield the filched token.

He came out of the entangled part suddenly and he knew at once that he had not come by the way he had entered. The murmuring voices were near at hand now and the human qualities were foremost, a man's low voice harping over and over on some senseless phrase, a woman's voice protesting in play and laughter. Then he saw that there were two people further toward the edge of the glade. Two clothed shapes, one dark and the other brightly flowered, moved together among the boughs. They were parting with caresses and promises, and when they were suddenly aware of him the girl was running away. Her flowered dress was sinking down the hill in and out among the trees and bushes. The light was on her head and then she was gone. Ben remembered her proud departure, her straight back and her lifted head, as if pride and daring had walked swiftly down out of the hill glade. He had seen enough of these two persons to know that they were lovers in the glade on love's business, secretly communing. The man had gone out of the place altogether. Ben did not know in what way he had gone.

He was surprised at coming thus out of the tangled glade where the bones had turned to white, unoffending lime. The lovers were gone quickly, but in the moment of their staying they had been abundant in life and feeling—words, hands, arms, cries, senseless phrases that were heavy with their meanings. They had made the flesh that would stand about the white, hard inner shapes, and in them it was quick and full. Their murmured words and sharp outcries covered the bones of men with a soft substance. He was abashed at what he had seen, and confused, so that he left the graves, even in thought, and he went to the creek-side where he searched for angle-worms. His mind was clouded over with a distaste for all that he had recently discovered, and he fished steadily, and was pleased when he caught a few small catfish. When he had spent several hours thus without pleasant thought, the cries of the lovers were subdued in his memory and he began to lose his distaste for them. He turned to the menace of the ants and he spent many hours trying to contrive a tight box that would preserve his food from them. Working at this, he went back to his first days along Elk Creek, to the first pealing of the bells, to the stalking giants in leathern clothing as he had thought of them while he explored the creek channel, to the great gods lain down at the edge of the sky, and to the two drab, mythical shapes bending to take a vessel out of the earth.

The days were long and slow, the nights short, the summer approaching midsummer day. Ben wondered now at the mental pictures he carried, pictures of a kettle being unearthed in a cornfield. He thought that some report of this vessel would surely be passing over the country, and he expected to hear of it when he went to the store in the village where he bought his food for cooking, but no word of it came to him. The men were busy in the fields, the season for plowing being at hand. Few came to the store to buy and none came to loiter. The storekeeper had little to tell when he was asked for news.

He gave little heed to the land about beyond his continual sense of it as being far-reaching and busy with life. He let the bells ring in whatever way they would without giving them direction or reason, nor did he know who lived in this house or that. He had written the names he had found on the tombstones into a little notebook with whatever dates he could decipher. Thinking with humor of the two clear drab figures leaning and bending above a hole in the ground, drawing iron and gold out in a great squat lump, he made a contrary picture arise—his family home in Jessamine County, his father and mother moving vaguely about in a house. He thought then that he would write a letter to his mother and ask her to send some of his clothing, but the kettle of this country continually forbade any other, as if it were sufficient for his musings, inducing idleness and dreaming.

Walking along the brow of a hill in the middle of an afternoon he measured his shadow as it walked stretched out beside him. It was long and lank like the ribbed sand after a sea-storm, and the legs of it, flung outward in a stride, were loose-jointed as if the bones of it were but lately assembled. On the horizon the hills were running in a long line, turning from the great sleeping god of the east to the lumpy beast that lay drunken or drugged in the northwest. A new query had come into his thought with his passage thus along the rim of a high pasture, and he asked what shape lies

behind the peal of a bell or the crowing of a cock,
the lilt of a donkey braying, and how this shape is
elongated, whether through time or space, or
both together. The bark of a dog merely stated
the question anew, the five tones of the peal
making five queries across the bright still air.
Walking thus he flung down from a high pasture
and strode through a rye field that stood waist
high and thence to a field of new corn. Full of
life, the herbs pressed upward, as if they would
lift him quietly forth. A midsummer quiet rested
over the hills, the growing herbs having some deep
business with what lay under the surface of the
soil, the growing herbs taking first place and con-
triving cunningly to have the best.

On a day late in the week Ben went to the village to buy food and he found several people astir
there. The buildings of the hamlet were gathered
along the one roadway and the street ran level
for a half mile or so between the tree-grown gar-
dens of the larger places and the close dooryards
of the cabins. At the end of the street there was a
small shop where tools and implements were
mended, and beyond this a few geese wandered
off with the turnings of a small stream. A hard

rain during the morning had brought an afternoon of leisure to the plowman, the ground being
too soft for working. The people, as they greeted
one another, spoke with pleasure of the rain,
taking the shower of the morning as if it were
theirs of some right, due them at last and somehow a credit to their good skill and their good
luck. At the shop there was a fervor of mending,
for the plows and the tools would be wanted for
the next working season. Men stood easily in the
door of the shop to talk together. They brought
their implements for mending, turning the mules
that conveyed these instruments in a wide circle
before the shop door, and they gave the tool over
to the mender with a careless inattention to
minute purposes and parts, as if they, as men, were
forever more than the machines they used. As
more, they walked away to the store to talk at the
doorway. They greeted one another with pleasant
banter, fostering old jokes, making subtle allu-
sions to old happenings in which all had shared
or about which all kept a common knowledge.
Toward the middle of the afternoon the space before the shop was cluttered with wagons or small
trucks or cutting instruments on wheels, but
presently, as the mechanic had tightened parts
or supplied bolts or screws or whatever was lack-

ing, only a few vehicles were left drifting in and out.

There was no knowledge of a kettle of gold among them. They had no peculiar news and no exciting matter to disclose or discuss. Their serious talk was of the rain and the fields, the state of the wheat and the fine prospect of the harvest.

Ben heard some people say that there was to be a party at Andy Blair's home on Saturday night. One or two said they had been invited and another, hearing of it, said that he intended to go.

"Old Andy himself invited me," a man said.

"Miss Philly invited me," one or two were heard saying. "Said a surprise would be there. I wonder what surprise old Mr. Andy could have to show."

"But you can't tell about a man like Mr. Andy. You couldn't tell what he might brood over and think out to surprise you."

Ben heard whispered surmises as to his identity. "A Shepherd . . ." one said.

"Some Shepherd come back . . ."

"I thought all the Shepherds were in the graveyard by now."

"The graveyard caught all the Shepherds a long while back. . . ."

They returned to talk of the party and all seemed to intend to go, some with interest, some with but a dull wish to be where others were assembled. Later a small quick woman came into the store and stood before the counter, and several other women stood close about her, looking at her, as if she were now famous and they wished to share in her reputation. She ran her small sun-browned fingers into the folds of some white cloth and disputed with the merchant, yielding to him just so far as he yielded to her. She laughed when a woman asked, "What's the news at your house?" and another woman laid a strong hand on her arm to detain her, and said:

"I'm so in a fidget to know I couldn't sleep last night, all the time in a wonder as to what Philly had to surprise a body with."

Knowing that this small woman was part owner and discoverer of the kettle, Ben stood back, away from the counter, to watch what she did. She had only a few small pieces of silver to spend, and these were knotted into the corner of a handker-chief until they were laid out on the counter and carefully divided, pushed here and there. If the needles were to cost ten cents even, there would be two cents more to go for the tea, she said, mak-ing this clear with her questioning and her quick fingers that shifted the coins rather than with her speech. There were smooth ripples and jerks in her clothing when she walked and her rough shoes tapped on the floor in a quick patter. Her face would be flung up quickly, her eyes shining in amusement or dispute.

"Are they to your liking?" the storeman asked of the needles.

"They'll do, but nothing to boast. It's been a good forty years since you saw a needle fitten to sew with."

When she was gone, the store being cleared, Ben came from the corner and bought a pair of shoe-laces, smiling within to see himself in this act, for he knew that he had no claim on Blair's party. But in the event that such a claim might arise, he ruminated, letting his inner laughter complete the condition; and he walked away from the hamlet staring down at his old shoestrings and judging them unfit for a public appearance. He turned out of the highroad, going west and south, and walked along a lane where the way dipped downward among cool green trees, and presently he saw that he would be overtaken by two riders. One was a lovely girl of nineteen or twenty who rode an old white mare, sitting sidewise without a saddle. The other girl was scarcely less lovely, and she rode a thin little gelding that was not broken to be bridle-wise, but was gentled by hard work in the plow until it obeyed her guidance without protest, although with awkwardness. They drew near slowly, coming from the rear, and Ben heard their voices speaking:

"I'm surprised already, Bonnie," the girl on the white horse said. "I'm already surprised enough."

"I'm surprised old man Andy Blair gives a party, let alone a surprise party," the other girl said, holding the thought forward for further consideration. Her voice was sweet and resonant and tender, like the voice of a coo-dove.

Ben had drawn aside from the narrow way to let the girls pass, lifting his cap. The girl on the white mare rode easily, her feet scarcely swaying with the rise and fall of the mare's back. Her flowered dress fell in soft ripples over the white hair of the beast and seemed of a kind with the snowy coat that spread to the animal's flanks and rounded over the plump haunches. This girl rode her beast with a stately grace, as if she rode to be crowned. She seemed faintly defiant as she passed. In three strides of the white beast she sat as if she were in some arrogant protest. Then her lips were parted, making ready for speech which was delayed by the act of passing. The other girl came forward, guiding her gawky beast aside to share the way, her pretty voice calling:

"Say, Robbie May, does Imogene take cream to Coulter's?"

The cry of the dove went over the lane and spread among the boughs of the trees. This girl moved quickly, asserting herself above her beast with a swift grace that flowed out of his awkwardness and brought it to a fine flower. They had passed then, the horses moving away with slightly accelerated gait, but they kept in view until the road forked, and then they went away into the hill toward the left. They had nodded slightly, seeing him stand out of the way as they passed. He gathered all that he could of them into mind as they rode forward along the lane, their light dresses, the up-and-down jog of a shoulder, the tones of voices calling out their sayings. He remembered one name, and knowing that the other name had been called he searched among the remembered lilts and soft words to restore it, and presently he had established it, Bonnie, as the name of the girl on the awkward beast.

After these girls, Robbie May and Bonnie, had left the lane, Ben cared no longer for it, and he turned his path into a field where he walked across sparse clover. Walking in the late afternoon sunshine he liked the country well then, and he liked all that it gave and all that it promised. These two, riding past him on their horses, had added a new content to the country, as a new fragrance or some fresh substance within the broad mass. Having lifted his cap to these two strange girls on the road, it seemed to him now that he must gain a name and a place in the community, to make what he had done have a part in neighborhood politeness, that he must become a part of the act already performed. He must have a house where he stayed and a reason for staying there. The flowered fabrics of the girls' dresses belonged to the ways of home and the life of houses. He felt suddenly unhoused, as if he were unclean and unfit. The cries of the girls' voices went over him with the slow rush and throb of the feet of the horses, gone now, but remembered. At the instant of this pleasant appearance, a foul thing came to mind, to convict him further. Unhoused and befouled, he recalled the pest that troubled his life in the open. The girls had made his need clear, they being still to the fore, and he remembered the ants and saw them running through their endless galleries under the ground.

"The little devils!" he cried out, and he leaned forward to spit far into the grass.

He saw their long hairy legs bent and crooked to make jointed parts, their round heads, their long slim upper portions, their wide, flat and rounded bellies. He saw the small, legless grubs, tended by the workers, the nasty little pupa cases opening to let the imago out. He spat them out mentally and cursed them with a momentary nausea. Standing on a rise of ground he put the ants out of mind and looked far and wide. The rim of the east hill lay along the horizon in rolling lumps and heaving masses—a great giant lain down to sleep at the edge of the sky. At the north another sleeper lay, stretched unevenly toward the northwest. His people—Tobias, John, Joel, John B. and Richard—all lay crooked and twisted and broken in a matted tangle of grass on a hill far to the right, but one foot-bone of them lay now in his pocket. He saw then that the world about Elk Creek and all the upper Pigeon River country had become finely settled and civilized. He had failed to note, he reflected, how richly the land had become inhabited, how the tracts had been broken up into fields, the wild beasts cheated and driven out, their dens broken open and cleared away. Houses, then, with men and women and girls inside them. All were looking forward to the harvest of the wheat. The people who had come to the hamlet during the afternoon were as actors in a show. A pleasant warmth spread over him when he restored the girls to the lane and saw their flowered skirts spread across the hairy backs of their beasts. When he had opened this vista again all seemed more clear, although he knew that but a few hired laborers would be wanted. But now that the wheat was ripening in the fields he thought that he might offer himself somewhere as a hand.

He was walking now far to the right and north of the lane where he had seen the girls, being far west of the main highroad. South of him lay the creek where he housed himself under the ledge, and to the right lay the Shepherd burying-place. He went outward through the fields. Walking thus he came to a house with its clutter of out-buildings, and as he came near the gate he saw that a man was walking about a barn enclosure, a ruddy man whose stride was long and whose way threaded in and out among the beasts there. His strong rough farm shirt was powdered with dust from the hay he had been stacking, and his hair lay in long pointed locks against his moist brow.

Ben stood at the large barnyard gate in respectful indifference and the man came forward after he had hurried his work mule through a rear gate and had given his sow a measure of corn. He knew that the farmer would surmise at once what he wanted, what he had come to ask. They stood at the gate and talked for a few minutes of this thing and that, not wanting to hurry forward the main point too suddenly, giving their minds time to gather all the threads of acquaintance before the mouth was let speak of the thing that was chiefly in mind. Ben said then that he wanted a piece of work with some farmer, enough work to help pay his way while he stayed in the country. The other was named Giles Wilson, he said. He had a farm-hand, and thus he did not need help for himself, and he asked Ben what kind of farm work he could do.

"About any kind," Ben said, "that a boy seventeen can do. Milk cows or shock hay. Run a plow. Sucker backer . . . Any kind."

Wilson said that he knew a man who needed a hand in a bad way, a man no longer what he used to be, heavy work now on hand with the wheat and the oats ripening. Then he went away, striding through the muck of the lot, and he cleared two pigs away from a trough where the calves should be eating and cuffed a mule out of the way of two humble nanny sheep. While he was striding about over the soft loam of the barnyard floor, Ben saw that he had fastened horseshoes to the soles of his shoes to save them from wear and he saw that his feet made horse-prints in the earth as he moved. He tramped about, setting his barnyard to rights, making an interval in which he considered Ben's claims. He cleared the pigs away with an angry hand, being puzzled, weighing all Ben had told him. He opened a door and went into his barn, but he came back presently and gave his cow a little rough fodder. Then he brought a bucket from the stones beside the well and, having washed the cow's udders, he began to milk her.

"What are you away from home for, this season, and work everywhere pressen?" This question came with the crying of the thin stream of milk as it struck the metal pail.

"I came here to get the dates off the tombstones over at the Shepherd graveyard," Ben said. "My father in a manner sent me. He wanted the dates and all the names. I thought I'd stay around a little while longer. . . . I had something on my mind . . . I wanted to see this country for a week or so. . . . And I'm not satisfied I got all the dates. . . . It takes time. . . ."

Wilson milked a great pailful of the milk and

set it aside. Then he turned to Ben and said, "You better stay all night."

Ben said that he would go back to his camp, that he had things there that needed looking after. He wanted to go to work the next day, Saturday, if he could. He wanted to be indoors before Sunday. He was thinking of the party but he did not speak of it, and when Wilson gave him a small pail filled with the freshly drawn milk he took it, still thinking of the party and seeing in Wilson a way of being introduced to the pleasures of the neighborhood.

"Bud Stoner, he's a good man," Wilson said at last. "He's the man I had in mind for you to see. Mr. Bud Stoner, he pays all he agrees on. I went by there today and I see Bud Stoner, he's about to get his house new painted. There's a sight of work to do there. Pays all he promises. You go see Mr. Bud Stoner. Go soon tomorrow morning."

Ben sat under his ledge during the cool of the evening, while the long twilight lasted. He adjusted his new shoelaces and he washed his clothes in the creek and spread them to dry on the bushes, his mind full of preparations, as if the eve of a new age had dawned. "I will arise and go . . ."

he said, singing or speaking. He had decided to apply to Stoner, to find himself a place in some house. He knew which house would be Stoner's. It stood back along the highroad, on the way to the hamlet, and thus nearer to the house into which the kettle of gold had been taken. The house holding the kettle must, indeed, be in sight from the upper windows of Stoner's dwelling, he reflected. He wished so earnestly that Stoner would give him work to do that he could not see any alternative, looking forward. He buried the trash from his camp and prepared the place for his final leaving.

There were lovely girls in his mind as the sunset faded, as the light slanted away from his small ravine and gave it an early night. He wondered, feeling again the nearness of the two, Robbie May and Bonnie, as they had passed him on the road, at the curious warmth that he had sometimes seen in the eyes of two, a girl and a boy, in the beginning of their kindness toward each other, and he wondered if this mark were ever upon himself. Then a fear arose within, and he thought that he would stay where he was and let well enough alone, turning straightway from this determination to contrive again, faint new desires arising. In his bold thinking he saw a long way ahead,

leaping over the difficulties that surrounded him,
seeing Robbie May and the other girl at Blair's
party; and he thought that if he might dance once
with each one of them he would be willing to ac-
cept his vacation as finished and call it well spent,
that he would be willing to go back to the place
from which he had come.

Early in the morning, before the cocks had finished crowing for the early hours of the day, before the farm bells had jangled and replied in
their sweet distresses and dissonances, Ben left his
half-cavern and walked toward the house which he
knew to be Stoner's, finding the owner of the
house, Stoner himself, just coming from the door
to make his way to the barns. When he offered
himself as a laborer he was told that there was no
farm work to be done that day, but that he might
paint the shutters of the house, and he was told
how to remove each pair, and where he would
find the green paint, and where he might stand
them for drying.

He sat with the farmer and the two house-
painters for breakfast in the kitchen porch. As he
settled to his seat and began to eat the rich hot
food he felt that he had come a long way, that

he had been diverted somehow from his intentions, but that presently all the frayed ends of experience would gather themselves together again. He had not thought of himself as spreading paint over wood. The farmer was a kindly, serious old man, gracious and bountiful. By the time all had eaten Ben knew that the farmer's wife, who came and went among them but did not breakfast at their table, was all but stone deaf, and that one painter was named Larkin and the other Grove.

He painted during the morning under the shade of a great tree, standing the shutters, one at a time, against the trunk of the tree and laying on the green paint carefully, teaching himself to be a painter. Grove and Larkin worked at the front of the house, or at the side, and they talked together, flinging out comments and reminiscences between long sweeps of the brushes and long periods of quiet. They seemed but little acquainted with each other, as if they had met only a day or two before, as if they continued confidences begun but a short time since.

From the lawn where Ben painted, the country rolled gently down, rising and falling with the fields, until it came to an abrupt end with the great, sleeping giant that turned apart, his head covered and his arms drawn under his shoulder.

Thus the country extended, going north and west. To the farther western point the farms dipped downward with the sinking bluffs of Elk Creek, but little visible from Stoner's lawn. To the southwest there was a rolling billowed field of wheat and beyond that the high parts of a cornfield and a vista reaching back between two hills that finally lapped together. At this point would stand the small brown house into which the kettle of money had been taken, the house invisible now, but some part of it would surely be seen from the upper windows of the wall above Ben's head. Beyond Stoner's the highroad curved and swept toward the north and the west and finally came to Wilson's gate, and Ben remembered Wilson's slightly stuttering speech, his long matted hair, his thrifty barnyard, and the horse-irons on his feet. The voices of the painters mingled with his sense of the spread of the farms, at first but little attended. They made a rough, broken comment, oaths and anger if a ladder slipped or took an unwanted position. Presently a voice came, standing clear of all the other sounds of the morning, one of the painters retelling something he had already made clear:

"Some days I used to knock down, anyhow, as much as six dollars above my wages," Grove said.

There was a long period of quiet, no comment offered, the brushes that slapped the house wall making the only sound. The morning was warm. The farmer was running a mower over a field of clover. The click of the cutting instrument came up from a farther valley field beyond the garden at the rear of the house. Grove made a lumbering noise lowering his scaffolding, and then his voice broke out on the air:

"But you couldn't knock down anything, systems they got now. Street-car jobs are a mighty poor make-out nowadays."

The doves in the trees sounded as if they were a long way off, making their coo-cries together. A cuckoo went into the dense foliage of a young sugar tree, assuming the motions of a snake as it went creeping through the air to penetrate the green banks of the leaves. Then Larkin spoke, his voice a sudden flutter of crumpled, unjointed phrases, a cracked voice uttering a crackling sound:

"Best knock-down job ever I had was ice-wagon job."

Regret stood about the house wall, another day having dawned. Grove daubed paint on the boards and spread it smoothly, making an even tattoo with his brush. Three times during the morning

they had agreed that everything was tight now,
nothing open and free, that the good day was past.
Coal wagons, ice wagons, street cars, wherever
money was passed freely, the new system was established over all as a blight.

"I only aim to work this job till I see something
better," Grove said. He spoke twice to Larkin's
once, as if he tried to convince the other. They
talked now and then of the paint and they poured
the mixture from one can to another, reaching
across from ladder to ladder. "Your sop's too thin,"
Grove said, pouring back into the other can.

"I said I thought it was too thin."

"When I paint, I paint. Whatever I do I do the
best I can. Don't put any more thin sop on this
house wall." They talked of the better mixture
and then slapped the brushes in a period of silence.

"Ever knock down anything while you painted a
house?" Larkin flung this query out in disjointed
caution, speaking in a low voice.

"Twice."

The morning continued, the farmer off in the
meadow with his clicking knives. The farmer's
wife hoed in her flower garden at the back of the
house, and there were no others about the place.
The windows were opened and the shutters spread
about among the trees. The cuckoo peered out

from its hiding-place and turned about within the dense leaves, its long tail like a sword against the limb of the maple. "Twice, I did," Grove said.

"Get away with it?" Larkin asked.

"Sure. I always get away with whatever I knock down. Easy if you know how."

There was quiet and talking alternating between them. The brushes worked forward steadily and the painters made the laps meet evenly, being particular with each board. The farmer's wife finished her gardening and presently she was walking about in the rear of the house and the kitchen yard, and a negress came from a cabin behind the garden to help her. It was after ten now, the morning moving slowly, but passing. Ben would make seventy-five cents above his day's food, for his work on the shutters. The labor of the field would begin for him the following workday, Monday, and he would sleep meanwhile in the farmer's house.

"Once it was twenty dollars," Grove said. "When I painted a man's store over in Bloomfield. Funny part was, nobody ever put any blame on me about it. . . . Other time was when I painted a roof for a rich old woman son-of-a-gun in Fayette County. Money saved up in a green teapot. Old woman so stingy she never missed it."

This reminiscence was contemplated for some

time in silence. The brushes worked lightly to finish the wall, and Ben wondered if he had heard the speech or had devised it out of the call of the cuckoo. It did not seem strange then that the bird might be crying out about a green teapot. The same voice offered then the last comment, spoken softly but with pride:

"You wouldn't believe me when I tell you it was three hundred dollars."

The shadows thickened for the noon of day and the cocks crowed from farm to farm, bringing an end to the morning. The farmer's wife tapped the bell in the kitchen yard and the flat metallic sound spread broadly over the farm to call home the farmer. Ben left his work and prepared himself for the table.

A table was set again on the kitchen porch and Stoner presided to serve and dine with his workers. The negress brought the food to the table, but Mrs. Stoner came to the door frequently to direct the work of the other woman. The table seemed crisp and fresh and clean, made thus by the neat starched cloth and the cool pitchers that collected drops of water on their sides, and the meal ran swiftly. Stoner engaged his painters in conversation, discussing the composition of good paint.

Larkin was bland and complacent, being willing to talk, but Grove assumed a knowing manner, as if he would not discuss paint with one out of his profession. Larkin's face was freckled and thin and his eyes were sharp and small. He would eat steadily for a short space and look up suddenly when he had thought of something to say. Grove had a large face, his lips large and uncertain. He would bite his teeth together and crumple the flesh beyond his mouth in a grimace that seemed to run with some inner hostile decision. He seemed unaware of the courtesies of a house. "Give me a biscuit," he said, when he wanted bread. He addressed his wants to the master of the house, ignoring the services of the maid.

Ben fitted the comments of the morning into their mouths, seeing them now near at hand. Behind his bland replies to Stoner, Larkin could easily say, "Best knock-down job ever I had was ice-wagon job," and his lips would fit tightly about the words that would come crumpled from one side of his mouth. He seemed pleased with his partnership with Grove, as if he meant to maintain it, and he would make light pleasant comment to turn Grove's sullen replies into a general agreement with what the master had said.

The negress went slowly about to pass the dishes

and the farmer's wife kept herself apart from the gathering at the table. Ben thought that she was being served in some inner room. As if some disagreement were being offered, Grove's jaws would be bitten together, and Ben looked at him to try to find out whatever pleasantness he might have, knowing that if he wished to court a friend this quality would appear.

"White lead, though, you can't beat lead for a basis for paint. To preserve wood . . ." Stoner said.

He had offered this opinion before, Larkin agreeing. "Always get away with whatever I knock down," as a manner of speaking, appeared before Grove's unfriendly silence, the large mouth biting into his bread. He had talked a little when Stoner had spoken of the hay, being willing to pass out of his own profession to make conversation. Back again on the matter of the paint, and he ate the food steadily, the flesh beyond his mouth settling to a hostile comment, the man actually silent.

After food and rest Ben went back to his work under the tree and the painters moved to the farther side wall to work. They seemed aware of him as they had not been during the morning, and their confidences were given in low voices. The farmer's cutting instrument made its pretty

clatter in the meadow, and the cries of the doves
broke now and then among the trees. The light
was hard and brilliant, lying densely over the
trees, destroying the shadows, and hard brilliant
insects leaped now and then out of the grass. Far
away to the east a rain cloud seemed to have gathered, but no cloud came here to the sky.

Ben heard the painters tell each other of the
party at Andy Blair's house. They had heard of it
at the village the evening before and they announced their willingness to go. Any small
pleasure that could be had in a country community was theirs of their right, they said, ex-
changing opinions that varied less than a hair's
breadth the one from the other. They always went
wherever there was a country party, they said.
They dismissed the party with but little comment
after Grove had said that he would go. Later they
came down from their ladders and mixed paint at
the rear of the house and Ben heard little of their
interchange. He spread the green paint on the
last of the shutters, working now in the mid-
afternoon stillness, for the cutting machine had
stopped for a period of rest.

There were bees in the air, and Ben thought a
swarm must be in motion, but he did not trouble
to find out which way they went. He spread the

paint in a half-dream, drowsed by the heat and the hour. The grasshoppers leaped out of the grass and dissolved themselves into grass again. When Giles Wilson passed in a battered car he stopped by the roadside and walked into Stoner's yard, bringing an end to Ben's drowsing. He looked at the shutters, being pleased that he had sent Ben there and pleased that Stoner had hired him, taking now an interest in the painting as of his right. He had been to town, he said, to the county seat. He made nothing of the heat, hot and cold, wet and dry, these being his daily wear. He carried a long crisp white paper which arose stiffly from his coat pocket.

"And what is this?" Ben asked, not minding what he asked him, moving swiftly into friendship.

"It's a pair of licenses, a pair of marriage licenses. Wheat harvest is a-comen on now and I didn't know when I'd get to town again, and Imogene says she'll have me. Imogene Cundy, that is. You wouldn't know her. And so I thought I'd get the licenses this time I was in town today, in case the time might roll around before I went again."

Ben asked leave to see the paper, drawing it from Wilson's pocket as he made the request. The shifting foot printed two hoof-marks into the soft path, and the hand, moist and red, but cool, gave the paper to be viewed. It was a marriage permit, prepared with decorum, founded in the law, waiting now to be served by some authorized person.

"But I have to run off with Imogene whenever I do it," Wilson said. "Imogene's daddy, old man Cundy, he won't let me set a foot inside the place. Run off, I've got to."

"What does Imogene look like? How does she look?" Ben asked then.

Wilson said he did not know. He stared off across the lower meadow and frowned and said "Shucks!" wanting to please his new friend and set Imogene before him, but he shook his head, as if words would not assist him. He said again, with a sudden smile, that he did not know. Changing the subject quickly he spoke of the party at Andy Blair's home, saying that it would be that evening. He would see Imogene there, he said, and perhaps he would name the wedding to her. Anyway he would show her the paper. He had caught up with his part of the work, he said. It was now Imogene's work to name what day she would run. It would be soon, in a day or two, or a week, maybe, and he asked Ben not to speak of it. He admired the green paint on the shutters and said that the house would be set off in a fine way when all was finished. He told again of the party and advised Ben to go, saying that everybody was invited. He himself was a distant cousin to Philly Blair, he said, remembering this suddenly, and he would get Ben a welcome. His face was round and smooth-shaven for the journey to the town, and a great flood of life beat under his skin, which was moist and clean and cool in its flow of sweat. When he was about to speak he would bring his face to a heaviness that was almost a frown, as if the matter under contemplation had not been given enough serious attention, but as he spoke he melted into a yielding gentleness. He was talking again of the party, looking forward to it. "It'll begin soon after sundown," he said, and he pointed the way to Blair's house. "You couldn't miss the place."

"Does she ever ride with two other girls, one on a white mare and the other on a two-year-old colt?" Ben asked.

Wilson said that she had no time now for riding, that he did not recall that she had ridden once during the whole summer. He took the paper again and settled it to his pocket, preparing to go.

"Early this week I saw a couple in the old graveyard. Would that be you and Imogene, maybe?" Ben made this a light matter, as if he were teasing.

"Graveyard? No. I haven't set foot inside the

graveyard this year. It wouldn't be Imogene neither."

"I just thought it might be, if her father is hard set against you. I saw a couple in the old Shepherd burying-ground."

"What couple?"

"A slim girl with a big-flowered dress. Went away fast when she saw me. A small slim girl. Big-flowered dress, green maybe . . ."

He shook his head and frowned, giving the matter heavy consideration. "Imogene, she's not small. Anyway it wasn't Imogene. I wouldn't name who 'twas." He settled the paper to his pocket anew and left with a sudden good-bye, clinking his irons on the stones by the gate.

Ben laid on the last of the paint, finishing his day's work. He touched neglected crevices and looked over the wood, searching for flaws in what he had done, and he felt a satisfaction in himself as a painter. His overalls were marked a little with the green but his shoes were free of it. As he worked now in the late afternoon stillness he summarized the week as he had passed it here in the Elk Creek country. Andy Blair and his wife, Philly, having found a pot of money, would have

all their neighbors in that evening to tell of their
good fortune and to show the unearthed treasure.
Two rogues, who filled in the time between their
rogueries with house-painting, would be present,
and they would undoubtedly have possession of
the money pot before morning, if it were brought
out to be viewed, or if it were merely announced.
The earth could scarcely hide so showy a loot as
a pot of gold but that they would uncover it once
they knew of it. He wondered what his own part
should be in the drama, returning to this difficulty
again and again after he had laid the matter aside
as beyond solving, ruminating the perils that lay
about the treasure. The weather-eaten stones in
the burying-place stood about, cluttered in the
bright light of morning or in the passing light of
dusk, dimly pictured now, and he remembered his
pride that there should be many there. The stones
had gathered up the whole past and stated it
briefly, running backward from himself to Tobias,
up and down in a line and widely spread in
branching streams. The pot of money came between himself and Tobias, put into the ground
somewhere between, and he wondered, asking himself again and again, who had buried it under the
tree and how the ancient owner stood in relation
to Andy Blair, and how he would look at Larkin

and Grove, and whose act, altogether, would make the greater roguery.

The air was heated now, the sun having penetrated all the shadows, the rays of light coming in hard slanted lines across the air. As he dreamed over the last of the shutters, touching unnecessarily at crevices, all the girls of the countryside went lightly across his mind, seen riding their horses or running away down a hill. He had held the papers of license in his hand, reading what was there defined, and he saw a dim appearance, a concept as of something sketched lightly at a long distance. Giles had said that he would have to steal Imogene when he got her, and he saw this care arise as a troublesome matter, full of risk and consequences. Neither of the girls who had ridden past him on the horses was Imogene nor the one seen running down the glade. Around Imogene gathered a warmth of risk and a future that was strange to foretell. It was pleasant to feel the delicate heat that she engendered. She with Giles would run out of some door and they would ride somewhere, and later there would be a minister or a magistrate to say a ceremony for them. He could not clearly see how these events would follow, one after the other. The girls who were not Imogene were like her in everything, perhaps, but widely divided from her now by the risk, by the paper Giles had brought from the county seat, and by the way of life that would follow her now and after. He placed them off, farther in the land, more distant than the one Giles wanted.

He laid on minute dabs of paint here and there, searching for crevices, trying to draw more near to the matters of his contemplation. He saw jealousy at a long distance, arising with hate and fear, not his own. Leaning over the painted wood to search it minutely with his brush, he felt the bone of his ancestor as it made a stiffness at the side of his thigh. They, these people, in the marriage license and out of it, seemed larger and more full than himself, more full of risks, having strange wants and curious needs put into their members. Imogene seemed the most rich in this. It seemed to him, dreaming, that it would be a pleasant thing to load risk upon her, to put upon her, to lavish, to spend, to take, to pile up, to make her the earth itself, to give to her, to plow her deep, to plant her with a harvest, to fertilize her with rain, to fling himself down on one of her cool hills in the shade.

He found that he was very warm, that the sun had penetrated the last of his sheltered places, coming horizontally now across the farmer's lawn.

He began to put the brushes away and to prepare himself for the day's end. He decided suddenly, being now awake and indifferent of what passed about him, that he would be, as formerly, a spectator to the show, that he would let the kettle of gold find out its own security and change hands as fate allowed.

The long twilight tarried among the fields, making more yellow the ripe wheat and putting a stranger green on the corn. Ben made his clothing neat, discarding his overalls, and he sat again at the farmer's table, seeing Grove and Larkin near at hand again. After they had eaten, Larkin brushed his hair carefully at the kitchen mirror and Grove came down the stairs in clean attire. Ben went away to his camp to secure the things he had left there, and he hid them more carefully under the brush, thinking that he would take them to the farm at some later time. This accomplished, he went toward Blair's home, approaching it slowly in the dusk, and, no others having arrived, he stood outside, hidden in the bushes.

A few hurried sounds came to him from the inner part of the house, and Andy came out of the house carrying a basket filled with yellow clay. There were sounds of a tool clattering on stones inside, and almost at once voices began to approach along the lane. Ben lingered outside to watch the people appear, a few coming at first, others following closely. Having passed inside, some of the visitors joked roughly with Andy and teased him to name his surprise. A large group of young people came, some of them singing, and while these waited about the door, Ben drew near and joined himself to them. The two girls who had ridden the horses came in this group, one called Robbie May and the other Bonnie, and presently he knew which girl was Imogene, hearing her name called.

Larkin and Grove came, walking boldly in at the door and seating themselves in a window where they viewed all that passed, looking both without the window and inside. Then Giles came hurrying from the way of the field, having walked from his farm. Ben greeted him and passed inside to be presented to the mistress of the house. He then went with Wilson to stand among the girls and the young men at the rear of the room.

III

CALLING OUT THAT SHE HEARD STEPS, PHILLY AD-
dressed Mr. Blair with deference and terror, but-
toning meanwhile her best dress. Wide extended
spaces, newly appearing in mind, reached and
spread backward from the little seed of her
thought where this one and that, her neighbors,
plucked at her knowledge, as if each one offered a
particle and took then his share of the accumula-
tion. The hot-weather locusts were crying out of
every rood of the extended land, but these points
of sound kept their fixed places, darting out from
the spread land as little spears of sound that went
continually forth and were continually present and
unspent. Beyond the fixity of the beetles and the
fixity of her neighbors as they were remembered,
the land wound and turned, drawing nearer to
wind her up into its strange core.

She could hear two or three speaking together at the door, and then others came. She hurried to the front room of the house, the parlor, and lit the lamps, one on the mantel shelf and the other on the dresser. She was trying to think of the trinkets put away among the mementoes in an old trunk up-stairs, thinking that she might find there some object which would delight or surprise, but nothing that she could remember seemed worthy of the gathering of people. She thought of a fine registered calf, devising the animal as she lit the second lamp, and she marked its brow with a heart-shaped white spot at the exact place where the little hairs turned about in a whorl. The calf yielded, pressed upon by the land outside, and she thought then of Susie and wished that she might ask assistance of her, for Susie, she reflected, had always been quick to think of objects and ways. The anxiety was dismissed with the memory that if she had nothing to offer she could give nothing more than the party itself, and the people might dance or sing or do whatever they liked and make sufficient entertainment of it.

"It's a free country," she said, muttering. "I don't have to have e'er a thing I haven't got and can't get nohow. It's a free country and that's all there is to that-there."

Callie Webster came, bringing two small children who ran curiously about, peeping behind shut doors and looking into hoppers and presses, spying out the place before they yielded themselves to it. Philly greeted her guests quickly, wanting to have done with it, seeing Andy move uneasily about among the people to make them a feeble welcome.

"What's happened to you?" more than one asked. "What's the good news?"

"Good-evening all," Andy said. His face was drawn tight with uneasiness. "Make yourselves welcome," he said, unevenly. "What's mine's yours." Or he called out in anger, "Here, you chaps, the party, it's not up-stairs. Come down from there. What you think you'd find up a man's stairs?"

The children came stamping down the steps and ran outside in their quest. "Callie's brats ever were a forward lot," a woman whispered near Philly's ear.

"What's the surprise?" two or three asked.

"Don't be in too big a hurry. Give Andy time. He'll name it in time."

"Did you, Andy, get a pension off the government?"

"Did you get a letter from your cousin out in Texas? The rich one, what's his name?"

"Or maybe he's got a nephew struck oil out west somewheres."

"Maybe hit's Andy's birthday. Maybe that-there's the surprise."

"Birthdays are no surprise. Iffen Andy brought me here over an old birthday I'd hold a hardness against him. Andy knows better'n to play on me any such trick."

"What's a birthday? I got a birthday myself last week and hit surprised me not one particle."

"Surprise is what I came here for. . . ."

A fine-mannered hush settled over the gathering, the first commotion of arrivals being passed. "Give Andy time. Don't crowd so. How could you expect Andy to name his surprise when there's such a rippet in your ears?" they were saying. The guests sat expectantly down into the chairs and polite inquiries and replies were passed back and forth. Then Andy came forward, striding crookedly in his best suit, and he placed Philly's chair over the hearthstone, testing the stone that rocked slightly underfoot. Philly was standing by the door, but she obeyed his command and took the seat he prepared for her.

"Let Philly sit in her usual place," he said. "Don't you, anybody, run into Philly. She's not so well today. I don't want Philly run into."

"What's got into Andy he takes pains over Philly?" one asked. "I never see old Andy so careful over Miss Philly in all my time afore."

Philly heard the voices, "Mr. Andy takes pains over Miss Philly tonight the same as if they got married only today. It must be their golden wedden. . . ." Others had come, young people coming together, coming singing along the lane. There was a throng assembled now, all the people of the near countryside, as many as the room would hold, the center of the floor being free.

Philly was sitting in the chair she used in winter when the fire burned on the hearth, but now she was placed so that she turned her back toward the chimney. Three women had found themselves chairs not far away, and the room, filled now with persons not commonly found there, seemed large and strange, reaching back from the three seated women, past the men who stood or sat beside the door and back further into the moving clutter of young boys. A boy opened his mouth to call out something but his words were lost in the noise. After he had spoken, Philly watched the up-and-down shapes and motions of his laughter when he joined his companions in the mirth he had made. Another boy held up his hands as if he made the shape of some object, showing its size, and Philly thought quickly of the exact size of the kettle and she knew that the object the boy defined was of a size twice as large. The dog tried to come in at the door but one of the women drove him out, saying that she could never rest easy to see a dog come into a house. All the people seemed at that time to be asserting themselves, having opinions and giving fixed shapes, as if they demanded something.

"I never could stand a dog inside the house," the woman said, seating herself again.

"I can stand a dog, but a cat is something I won't abide." One or then another was speaking.

"It's sad about Imogene," the first woman said.

"When a girl's father is hard set against her sweetheart, it's a sad time, unless she's hard-hearted, and Imogene is not."

"It's a hard thing when a girl no older than Imogene has got to make a choice between her own father and another."

It seemed then as if the demands of these women passed, flowing into some liquid pity, when they talked of Imogene. Philly allowed the woman her prejudice against the dog and she saw clearly at that moment how a great beast, giving ill odors to

a room, might be undesirable. She saw why the
other might not like a cat sneaking about inside
a house. She joined them mentally in their pity
and when the first woman said again of Imogene
what she had said before, Philly nodded her head,
gathering all that was said into a yielding sorrow
for which some redress must be found after a
little.

"It's a sad thing about Imogene. It's not like
Imogene neither, to meet a man out somewhere
else on the sly."

"Men are a strange race. Not like women. It's
curious now."

"A strange race, they are, but what other kind
is there, beside women?"

"Sometimes you hardly seem acquainted with
the man you're married to twenty years, and all
the time you know every thought inside his head
and every act his body can do or is likely ever to
do. And there he is, strange. So strange you wonder sometimes if it's a man or a horse or a hay-
bailer or what kind anyway you're wedded with
all your life."

"I said that to myself all the way on the road
here tonight. But what other kind is there?"

They were making hard shapes again, as if they
demanded something which was not visible. Philly

leaned back, away from them, resting her shoulder against the top of the chair. She remembered then the two pearls in the little tied-up pouch and remembered that Andy had made a secret of them, that he had hidden them even from her.

Callie opened the organ and began to play a march, filling the whole house with a great leaping of noises out of the reeds, the time beaten with the windy pedals that sucked at the air and blew up the music or let it fall away from moment to moment. The player pulled out other stops and the music became hollow and thin and leaped about as if it went off among the stairsteps, or other stops again, and it surged with a brassy clatter, and all the people shuffled uneasily in their chairs and moved slightly apart from the places where they had been, making sinister faces. Philly saw that music is a strange sort of thing and that men are strange, and she reflected that music and men have a strangeness together. Then Callie changed the stops again and blended the noises in some more accustomed way, the march rhythm still beating through the reeds.

Philly sat firmly over the hearthstone as Andy had placed her, her eyes darting about over the

company, her feet pressing the place that covered
the pot of money. She named the people as she saw
them, calling mentally each one, as "There's Effie
Trigg and there's her aunt, Hester. Robbie May
Rudds could take time from her courten to come;
and look at Ed Sims, got on a suit of clothes.
There's Hez Turner; I didn't say to invite him
neither. . . ." Back in the throng she saw the
strange young man, the one Giles had brought to
speak to her. He was one of the Shepherds, of
whom there were many in the graveyard. She
thought of him now as a part of what cluttered the
room. He leaned against the wall, his shoulder
drooped to meet the flatness of the plaster, and
he talked with Robbie May and Bonnie when
they stood near. She saw him watching two others,
strangers who sat together in a window, and she
turned to the nearest woman to ask who the
strangers were. Hearing their names and that they
were house-painters, Philly wished them gone
when her eyes roved over them again.

They were a pleasant gathering then, all seeming glad to be assembled. Philly wished in this instant that she had thought to have a party before a
kettle of gold had come into her knowledge. The
people seemed to be making sufficient happiness
for one another. Hester Trigg, a blooming, hearty,

pink-cheeked woman, sat in the largest chair near the middle of the room and she seemed to be reaching out to gather everything in. She sat resting happily as if she managed all that went forward and all was going to her liking. When she said "Sing Beulah Land," Lester Rudds hurried over to the organ to sing it, and when she said that the lamp was smoking, old Mr. Bonnie turned the wick down for her and was glad that she had found a thing for him to do. Andy and another had reached toward the lamp, but old Bonnie was more quick. Andy had not wanted to invite her because she was a widow. Her glossy stockings were smooth over her plump ankles and her great body was neatly stayed to the shape she desired. She smiled easily and looked at all with a big, easy kindness which meant that she understood whatever it was that ached inside them. Her quick breath came and went freely, and she fanned herself with a folded paper, flapping it sharply back and forth. The people were still making pleasures for one another. While Callie's music shuffled at a march again, Bonnie and one of the young men began to dance, holding each other and taking little steps that scarcely moved them over the floor, shaking their shoulders to the rhythms Callie made, and Robbie May danced with another, using the same little steps. They moved out to the bare space of the floor and circled about.

"Make these young scallywags quit their devilment," one of the women near the organ called out. "It shames me to see what the world's come to. It shames me to sit still here and look at what I see."

"Do you see harm in dancen?" Bonnie asked. The steps went forward in wormlike procession, and the music continued. Andy walked uneasily about while the dance lasted, and if he passed near Philly he inspected her feet as they were set down on the hearth. "No matter if there's not a chair to furnish every one," he said to Ronnie Rudds. "Philly is right tuckered out and might as well sit down and take her ease."

Philly leaned back to ease herself, letting the party take whatever turn or form it would, letting the dancers have the event. Their dancing was of no moment to her now, it being no matter of importance whether young men and girls whirled or glided or bobbed about today or yesterday or tomorrow. She could arise from her chair and dance with them, but her movements would have been of a swiftly whirled sort. In herself she felt the sum of all that the dancers were, and she clicked her tongue at what she felt. Robbie May had a circle of bright beads about her neck and her pink dress made a spot among the turning clutter of the young men whom she chose or rejected according to her pleasure. Tomorrow she would be feeding her fine baby beef the balanced ration as the farm agent advised, and she would go to see Bonnie's calf to see if it were growing as fast as her own. Effie Trigg was plump and large-built, and back of her lay a cushion of easy living where she took her beauty sleep unhindered. She was of a kind to take all that she wanted and to be wanting freely. Giles stood taller than the other young men. He seemed troubled, and now and then he would bite at his lips, as if he had not clearly made up his mind what to do next. His hair lay on his forehead in three pointed locks, and Philly said of it, "Iffen he waits to get it cut after wheat harvest it'll be a sight." When there was dancing Giles would step out onto the floor and fling a few measures with his feet, as if he would like to have done with trouble, as if he would like to shuffle his cares away.

Imogene had come quietly in at the door, being shy of the gathering, and she had stood since the beginning of the party with the other girls beside the wall. Her face was plump and round, but white with the pallor of one who stays much in-

doors, for her labors allowed her to go out of the
house but little. Philly had a pride in her whiteness, as if it marked her for a lady, and she wished
for a fine satin dress to put upon her in order that
the signs of gentility might be made true. While
Imogene talked now and then with the girls who
stood about her, Philly looked at her soft white
face and she knew that if there were tears to run
down her cheeks they would be large, full round
globes that would gather slowly and fall slowly
down. She was full-chested and strong, slim at the
hips, and Philly had a sudden confusion, as if she
did not know clearly whether this girl was Imogene or Lispy, her mother, and when Imogene
rested her head against the wall behind her for
an instant, Philly thought that Lispy had come
back to stand in her parlor, and she half rose from
her chair, feeling a down-dragging motion at her
chin as if she were about to cry out. Lispy had
been dead seven years or more. Then Philly saw a
clear shape, evenly defined and sharply rounded;
it was the hold Sam Cundy had on Imogene and
the reason for his hard demand, shaped now to
a conclusion in her mind, as clear as if she saw a
pictured object. Cundy wanted to keep Imogene
in his house. He would never consent to have her
marry. He wanted her about, under his eyes, near

his hands. She looked like her mother; he held her confused with the other woman in his mind; he would not let her go.

She seated herself easily again, letting the shapes and images that had troubled her lie unattended, and she leaned against the back of her chair again. The woman beside her was speaking:

"I never could stand a dog inside a house." She had risen to drive the dog away.

Philly leaned near the woman suddenly and asked:

"What would you do iffen you had a crock full of money suddenly come to your hands?"

"What? . . . Why a crock full?"

"Well, a pan full then? What would you do?"

"I'd say, 'Lawsie goodness!' . . . How much would be in the pan full?"

"Say a thousand dollars, and maybe more."

"Hear Philly talk! Whoever saw a thousand dollars in a tin pan? Or in a crock either? I don't know what she means."

"Money is not so easy got together as that," the second woman said. "How could you ever keep it together long enough to make a crock full?"

"That's hit. And if you found hit together in a crock how long would hit stay there?"

"That's what I wanted to know," Philly answered her, sharply. "That's what I asked first-place."

"It's past belief. There's no such crock. I never in all my days heard of it."

"But if there would be such a crock," Philly said, "would you be glad to see it? To set your eyes on it once?"

"I'd say a crock's not a safe place to keep money in. I'd want it locked away tight when night comes. I read a piece in the paper yesterday about a woman and she kept her money in a blue teapot."

"It was a green teapot. I read that piece myself. It was green, Eliza."

"And what happened?" Philly asked.

"Somebody stole out of it. Left the teapot there but took out the money."

"It happened a right smart while ago but was found out only the other day. Took the money out, but left back the teapot, empty. It was a little piece away down in the corner of the paper. . . ."

While the woman spoke the last, her right eye twitched and became weak, as if she saw the shape of the teapot, the money all gone out of it. She was the same woman who had taken Lispy's promise, who was unable to fulfill it, whatever it was. Philly drew back from her and rested herself more easily in her chair again, wanting now to withdraw from the woman's spent and ineffectual present, and remembering her own promise to Imogene she pressed her feet more firmly down on the stone.

Three men sat beside the door, drawn together to talk in low tones. They were hardly aware of the rest of the gathering, but they talked of their cultivating and offered arguments back and forth to prove the virtues of deep plowing or shallow, as one or the other was convinced. In their talk the fields came near the door and the spongy loam gave out moist odors, as if it were not darkened now by the night and lit by the moon. "I always tear in deep, to the roots of my corn," one said; but another, "Plow shallow, I always say. I'll tell you what I've seen in my time"; or another, "You take a ten-acre field . . ." Hearing these words Philly had another desire in mind, sharp-edged—the beginning of a new day, the coolness of early morning when the body was full of the unspent food that had been eaten, when the horse was dragging the rake off toward the new-cut field, himself full of his fodder and eager for labor. The little pigs would be crying out their pleasure over their mash. She wished for day and for these pleasures, and for the labor of the harvest; she wanted sleep and the quiet of the night so that in the end she would be hurrying out to tend the little chickens. The voices of these men did not at any time blend with the clatter that was passing over the room, but they floated with the morrow and the outside where the beasts were now sleeping, where they rested for the coming of another day.

One of them talked of the power of the light moon over the dark one and told of signs, or another recounted the virtues of sprays and of terracing for the saving of hillsides, one holding to the new way and another to the old. Their words lay now under the general confusion and were never lifted above it, but came clearly when the din broke apart and burst into nothing. Callie had finished the piece she was playing, and there was a lull of the windy music, but the rhythm went over the room, kept unbroken while the music rested. The rhythm was continuous, beating about, and one or two beat their hands together, or they tapped the floor, and when Callie played again she but fitted the throaty measures of the organ to what already pulsed. The young people seized the rhythm again and danced upon it, making their bodies quiver, or they sang brief phrases, looking at one another with kind eyes.

Effie Trigg was everywhere, beside the organ, beside the hearth, or she was with the girls at the farther side of the wall. She was continually laughing. Every small motion of being, whatever its kind or temper, became a matter of laughter when it passed over her. There were little dimples and creases beside her mouth, and it was pleasant to see them move when she said something and went at once into fresh laughter. The flesh of her arms seemed to laugh as her arms shook with the quivering of her chest. Her fat hips laughed and her round knees.

"Oh, it's harm to dance," one woman said. "Devilment, it is. Look at Bonnie."

Giles Wilson leaped out into the floor and began to prance to the music. He came back to his place beside the wall and stopped beside Imogene and Robbie May, but made another sally about the floor and a prancing step beside the girls.

"I don't care one which nor whether if I dance or not," Bonnie said, answering the woman. "I just thought I'd dance a little, while I waited for Mr. Andy to name his surprise."

Then Effie Trigg began to shake with the

rhythm of Wilson's dance, and she offered herself, laughing until the creases about her mouth
broke into newer ripples that were pleasant again
to see. Ed Sims set his hands firmly upon her
plump shoulders and they began to bob across
the floor. Sims laughed with her, and Wilson,
moving about them, dancing alone, laughed too,
until a new laughter came to his face, a kind that
seemed to be of a more deep and thorough mirth
than any Philly had seen on any face before. Effie
Trigg was abandoned now to a deep shivering
laughter, and while Sims bobbed with her about
the floor, Giles seemed about to take her from the
other. This dance came suddenly to an end with
the break Callie made in the music, and she
turned about from the keyboard to rest herself.

The dog had come in unnoticed and it had lain
for some time on the floor not far from the door.
When Giles left the floor the dog arose and went
toward the hearth, sniffing at the boards; but suddenly it leaped forward and began to claw at the
stones, bounding about, and Philly could scarcely
push it away from her feet.

"It's a rat he smells," Rudds said. "I never saw
a dog so keen after a rat before." There was a great

deal of laughter at the eagerness of the dog. They were making opinions:

"Look at that dog . . ."

"I never could stand a dog to come inside the house . . ."

"There undoubtedly must be a varmint under the floor, the way he tears at the boards."

Andy put the dog outside and closed the door, and the people forgot him in a moment and turned back to their pleasures again. Giles leaped once more to the floor and he pranced alone, as if he would start more dancing, but Hez Turner and Rudds drew near the organ and called for songs that were sung in the church, saying that they would have a singing. Then the pulse that poured over the throng was used for religion, and a great throbbing revival singing leaped to the ceiling and beat up the staircase and shook the pictures hanging above the organ. Imogene moved timidly about near the wall, passing the two house-painters who sat in the window, and she came at last to the hearthstone and stood beside Philly, inquiring after her health.

"I'm afeared you might be sick, Cousin Philly," she said. "You don't look so well as common." Her feet were beside Philly's feet, the stone moving a little under their weight.

"It's about time Andy named his surprise," a man said. "I'm ready now to hear what the good news might be. Bedtime is not far off, and I'm not of a mind to sit up tonight."

"Yes, that's hit." There was a clamor, wanting surprise.

As if to add weight to these demands, Callie set forth on a long jiglike song which none sang, and Turner, the evangelist, stood near the wall, nodding his head to the tune in apathetic hostility. Robbie May and Sims began to dance in their corner, and a woman leaned near to Philly and cried out:

"It's a sin to dance to organ music. I'm surprised the floor, it won't open and swallow us all down inside."

"I'd be afeared somebody might die in family iffen I danced right on top of church music. It's time Andy told what his surprise is. Unconceal what 'tis. We're a good deal out of patience to wait longer."

Philly was thinking that the party had lasted a long while. The time seemed long since Andy had given her the seat over the hearth, and she asked Imogene to tell her the time by the clock above on the mantel. But an hour had passed. With the demands of the last speaker she had begun to think that she would ask Giles and Imogene to help her prepare a surprise. She began to think of Imogene as one of very great importance, as if she were more than all the others present, as if her likes and dislikes were in some manner hallowed and her need to be gone from her father's house were immediate. The intended marriage of the lovers turned about in her mind and seemed imperative. She assailed it with her own necessity in mind, to see if she might devise something for herself from it. She wanted to take Imogene into her arms and rock her on her small bosom, and while she held the girl's hand, Giles came from among the boys and stood next to her, and it seemed to her then that some news or announcement might be made of the intentions of this pair. It seemed clear to her then that some news or secret disclosure might be made of it, and she began to enjoy the party and to be glad the people had come. The men about the door were talking now about the prices of land and the value of this or that tract, of how much oats a man ought to get from a certain high field. Several were dancing in a far corner, all the groups following their likes and all awaiting and demanding. She whispered with Imogene, beginning to tell her that the surprise she had planned had not turned out well, that she would have to

find another, and Imogene was troubled to hear
her say this. Imogene's concern was a pleasure to
her, as if she herself had now an ally. She became
careless and bright, enjoying the party, yielding
much of her concern to Imogene's distress. Then
Giles gave her a stiff paper to hold, saying as he
dropped it into her lap:

"Take care of my paper for me, Miss Philly.
I'm bound to lose it or drop it underfoot, one. A
pair of licenses for me and Imogene I got in town
today."

Philly fingered the paper and when she saw that
it was of great importance she closed her hands
firmly over it and pressed it securely together. It
was the binding string that held Giles, and she
shook it in her fingers. He might wander a little
way into Effie Trigg's mirth and her sluttish dancing, but she would beckon him back with one jerk
of the crisp document. The three of them, Giles,
Imogene, and Philly, were leaning together, whispering.

While Philly sat thus bending toward Imogene
to whisper, she felt a movement thrust upward
toward her ankles, as if a hand were reached up
from the hearth below. She drew back suddenly
and she saw the dog's head at the hem of her dress.

He was sniffing at the hearth at her feet, insistent now although she pushed him away. The people near were curious of the dog and they said again that there must be a varmint hidden under the floor. "Hit's a polecat," one said. "I can smell hit myself." Some of them were sniffing at the air then to test it for signs, but many were uncertain of what they smelled. The dog continued to paw at the floor or the stone, and several came forward to watch what he did. Giles dragged the dog outside, but the boys were curious now to know what was under the floor and why the dog wanted to tear up the hearth.

"There's a polecat under the floor," the painter, Larkin, said. Both painters came forward with the crowd that gathered about the hearth. The young man, Shepherd, stood to the fore, near to Larkin. He sniffed the air and said he did not smell anything unusual, and while he said this he looked like old John B. Shepherd as Philly remembered him, but far younger, having a lank chest and a loose-jointed stride. Old John B. had been in the graveyard thirty years and Philly took one instant from her fear for the kettle to wonder at the likeness that stood before her.

"If you want us to get that polecat out, Lady, we'll open up the floor and put all back," Grove said to Philly. He was standing up before her, looking at her with loose, large-lidded eyes, his large mouth chopping up and down over his words. "Let's get the varmint out for Mr. Andy and Miss Philly," two or three called out. The party swayed, all the young men crowded near the hearth to sniff at the air.

Larkin and Grove and Ed Sims pressed forward through the young men. Grove had now brought an ax from the yard and Sims had brought Andy's pick. Philly had known Sims since he was born, but only now she saw that he had grown to be a brawny man of a great size. She had not seen that he was growing, but now the pick seemed to be a toy in his hand as he tossed it lightly, and he was telling meanwhile what should be done, his great arm-muscles leaping in little jerking movements as if they laughed together and were eager to show their force. The boys were making a great joke.

"It's a rat, that's all," a boy said.

"No, hit's a weasel." They were contending and laying a bet.

"My twenty-five cents says it's a rat."

"Thirty-five cents says it's not anything at all," Sims called out.

"Four bits says it's a polecat."

Philly spoke out then, forbidding anyone to

tear up the boards. She could scarcely hear her own voice in the din. Callie had left the organ, and some of the women were telling the young men to let the floor stay, that Philly did not want her house torn out during a party, but the arguments were feeble beside the betting. Andy came a little way into the crowd, being pushed this way and there by the young men who were eager to be near the hearth, and the coins of the bets were held up in their hands. Philly said again that the boards of her floor would not be broken away, that she did not want a hand to tear out one single plank.

Then one of the strangers was standing before her, turning lightly about with the rest and coming to a stand directly before her knees. The strangeness left him and he seemed familiar, as shaped to meet some picture slightly different from the one her eyes reported. It was old John B. Shepherd, with loose-fisted arms dangling, and a big-boned, flat-shouldered twist to the easy hardness of all the length of him just under his neck, with no stomach to speak of where the ends of his chest crumpled together to make ready for his narrow hips. It was old John B. turned young again, got out of the graveyard and gone back into some time behind Philly's memory when he might have

been a growing boy with a clean face and plenty of
hair on his knotty head. He had the old John B.
smile that accompanied old John B.'s little-dis-
played goodness of heart and interest of mind, for
old John B. had kept free of the drag of pity and
had eased himself and hedged himself behind
irascibility. He was standing in the thick of the
young men but he was not making a bet. He made
a gesture with his hand as if he wished Giles Wilson to come and stand beside him. Philly remembered him as being much older than herself, as
being at one time the teacher at the school when
she was a beginner there, as mumbling Latin
names for things, as taking long strides out to the
field where the grown boys played and turning
little Elijah Wilson over in his haste. He was smiling now, and the corners of his lips went up while
the sides of his cheeks went down, and then the
center of his mouth twitched forward as if he were
undecided whether to whistle or to sing. He made
a gesture inviting Giles to come and stand beside
him while he smiled and grinned, as if he cared
only a little whether the boards were lifted or not,
and he was saying:

"The lady says she doesn't want her floor torn
up."

"Stand aside. We'll put back all we rip up,"

they were answering him. "The boards are in a manner loose. They'll come up and go right back. No trouble."

"If a lady says, 'Don't tear the floor out,' you can't do it, can you?" Shepherd was speaking to Sims and the other young men, turning away from the house-painters. The boys had pushed nearer and the men were falling back, careless and ready for some other diversion. Lester Rudds called for another song, wanting to stop the noise before the hearth, to turn the whole gathering about a song he had chosen, and he asked Callie to come back to the organ and play for him. One or two standing apart agreed with Shepherd in what he had implied in his question to Sims, and these went further back out of the crowd, saying the same thing in different ways, but Sims called out:

"A varmint is a dangerous thing to every hen-roost in the whole country. It has to be killed, no matter whose woodpile it hides under. That's how I've always heard it said." He was laughing; he had made a bet that there would be nothing under the boards.

"But if a lady says, 'Don't tear out my floor,' it's good manners not to tear it out." It was a curious thing to hear old John B. saying this; it was the kind of speech he used to make in the schoolhouse

and Philly then had held a little slate in her hand.
Now and then he would begin with a fresh beginning, as if old bygones and old stupidities were to
be forgotten: "Now, boys and young ladies," he
would say, "we have for our consideration here
today words of two syllables accented on the first,"
and all would begin to say or to sing,

> b..a..ba k..e..r..ker baker;
> l..a..la d..y..dy lady.

Philly rubbed the old, unwanted words off her
slate with her moist hand and Eliza Rudds was
jostling her arm so that she could scarcely write.
"We have for our consideration here today," making a new beginning. Shepherd was speaking still
to Sims and to the other young boys who stood
about the hearth. "That's how I always heard it
said. If a lady says, 'Don't tear out my floor,' it's
good manners to leave it be." He was laughing
now, as if he did not care what they did, and he
let himself be pushed here and there, but in the
end he was in his place before Philly, and he did
not move far when one tried to push forward and
make the first eagerness for the upturning of the
boards come back to the throng.

Sims smiled a long slow smile, and he flung his
pick out at the door. "If Miss Philly, she don't

want her floor opened we won't tear out e'er single
board," he said in a great voice, his long stout
arms reaching about. "Like the strange boy says,
it's not in good manners to go against a lady in her
own house. We'd best heed Miss Philly here." He
reached for the ax and flung it outside the door,
and he cuffed the dog out, closing the door tight.
"No matter if there's lions and tigers underneath
the floor," he said.

Philly saw that the floor would not be opened
and the disturbed hearth revealed, and she was
glad with a brief rush of thankfulness. "Those boys
have got a blight on themselves, to want to bet on
every least thing," she said to Imogene. "It happens like that when you invite your house full, a
part bound to be white-trash." Thankful, she sat
quietly back for a little and measured the passing
of the night by the oil in the lamps. The bowls
were half full and the chimneys were smoked deli-
cately over with a faint film or cloud where the
wicks had been too high at the beginning of the
evening. Measured by the burning of the oil the
evening was more than half done. Her pleasure
that the crowd of boys about the hearth had been
dispersed settled to a fixed anxiety when she saw
that Andy was in a tremble for what had happened, and she tried to make him go outside,

gesturing with her hand, but he would not leave. The evening was more than half spent; the lamps announced this to her; she knew now that she must turn her mind to devise some amusement for the gathering or pass this matter by altogether and say quietly that she had nothing.

Some of the women had joined Rudds and called for more singing, and Callie spread a new song on the organ, one from the book of exciting songs used for revivals, and the singers gathered near. The music leaped up swiftly, once Callie had started it, the rhythms used now again for religion, and the song was like a quick chariot that rolled over the air. When the song was making a din, Philly drew Imogene near, and Giles bending toward them, she began to ask them to devise some entertainment with her, some announcement that would satisfy the gathering.

"Would it be enough to be called a surprise iffen you and Giles let it be known you have it in mind to run off and get married tomorrow or next day?" Giles thought it would not be enough, and Imogene said that she would then be afraid to go home for the night, that her father would be sure to hear of it. Philly pushed the matter nearer, asking them if they could run off that night and if one day were not as good as another when it is marrying that is considered. She proposed to them that they go now, that they leave her to announce their intention after their leaving. Nothing seemed clear. Imogene was confused and but half willing to this. Philly proposed another way, and another. They continued to whisper together.

Philly looked up from speaking with Imogene when she heard the song mount to a great volume, for a dozen people were singing with loud voices. Hez Turner was beating the time with his hands, himself riding on the power of the song, and he began to admonish with a loud voice, his phrases thundering with the rolling song and making terrible warnings and judgments that seemed to be falling from the leaping music. He was mistaking Andy's distress of mind for a distress of spirit, and he began to address himself to Andy, admonishing him.

"I do believe Andy, he's about to get Hez Turner's religion," Eliza, one of the women sitting near, was saying. She leaned forward and tugged at Philly's sleeve, and she spoke as if she gave a warning. "Philly, honey, I'm afeared so."

Turner flung out his long, accustomed chant, his eyes on Andy's face, and his hands were sweep-

ing and pointing through the air close before
Andy's gaze. Philly shifted her feet about to break
their stiffness, and she saw prayer and singing confused, Turner's voice being lifted continually
above the song. She saw Andy groan and beat the
air with his hands and she saw that the buried
kettle of money was not yet free from menace.
Andy was weeping and tearing at his coat, reject-
ing Turner's discipline, shaking his head, but
Turner pursued him, crying over him, "It's your
pocketbook is your stumbling block. Lay your
whole pocketbook on the altar!"

Some of the people were watching Andy closely,
but some were indifferent, and these sat apart to
talk of their own affairs, being well used to Turner's ways. "A party ever was a hard-to-manage
thing," Philly said to Giles. She held tight to the
marriage paper, closing her hand over it more
firmly when the new fear arose. Wilson was speaking near her shoulder:

"I'm bound Hez Turner, he'll get every cent
Mr. Andy has got. He's a master hand to make a
man give up his pocketbook and all he's got saved
by."

"I've noticed a change come over Andy here of
late," a woman cried out, bending near. "He's as
apt as not been in mind to try Hez Turner's reli-

gion, worried and all. As apt as not that's what his
good news is about."

"It's not, though," Philly said back to her. "And
I'll not have Andy worried. Hez Turner can take
his religion away and leave Andy be, and you can
tell all I said so."

She arose from her chair, but she remembered
Andy's admonition that she sit so that her skirt
would hide the altered stone, and she sat in her
place again. Turner had pressed Andy down to his
knees and he was bending over him, crying out his
continual advice, "Lay your whole pocketbook on
the altar." This phrase beat over Andy continually
and he was thrusting at the air with his hands, and
she wondered if he thought then of the kettle or
of the little sack in which were hidden the two
pearls, and which he would give. Callie had
brought the song to an end, but the singers were
selecting another and were beginning to sing, for
they were but little concerned with Turner's admonitions. The men beside the door were talking
and thus a level voice ran under the commotion
in the farther corner. "You let me have four
bushels of good clover seed . . ." The admonitions of the fanatic burst over this speech about
the clover and ran above it, but when the high
voice was done for the moment the quiet voices

were saying, "Orchard grass, though, I take a heap of stock in orchard grass. . . . Or you take timothy . . ."

She began to whisper hurriedly with Imogene and Giles, the voices of the men making her know that she must do something quickly, now, before tomorrow should come nearer. She had a fear that Andy might yield to the exhorter, that he might buy relief and fling open the hearth to bring forth the kettle, that he might fling the gold and silver pieces over the floor and shout, "Take all . . . God's sake! Everybody take!" She plucked Imogene's sleeve in her distress and drew her arm nearer, the men at the door talking of tomorrow and bringing tomorrow nearer with their talk about the clover seeds and the cuttings of timothy. She did not wait now for arguments, but made her opinions stand out as necessary, urging and hurrying:

"It would be a surprise a-plenty iffen you stood up now and got married," she said. "And Turner here to say the words and the ceremony. As well now as tomorrow or next day. Why not? Here's everybody at hand and no secret, witnesses a-plenty and the license papers all ready. . . . Offer Hez Turner three dollars, spot cash, and see how quick he'll let Andy be, or whatever ready money you've got in your clothes. . . ." She needed to urge them only a little for they were now more than half willing. "As well here as somewhere else later, off in town somewhere," Giles said. They gathered more nearly together under Philly's urgent whispering and withdrew to a more light whisper which she could scarcely hear, their wishes arising to meet her wish. The steady talk of the doorway continued, flowing now about some low-spoken things, the nodding of heads accompanying what was said, and Philly felt at ease. She was calling Rudds and making known what would follow, asking him to stand forth and announce that there would be a wedding. Then Rudds's voice began to grow out of the noise, a hush falling slowly. The voices fell away as if a swift rain had blown over, and one patter of words after another ceased. Giles and Imogene were still speaking together, heard again now at Philly's shoulder as the sounds of the room fell away:

"You could come with me tonight to my house," Giles said. "I had a woman, old Mrs. Rudds, come over one day this week and make all fitten for a lady."

"And of a morning I could help you milk the fresh cow, so you could get to the field soon after

sunrise. And raise the little pigs on the skim, like
you ought to. . . ."

"The sow littered today, for a fact she did, and
it's as much as a man can do to keep the field work
in hand. But tomorrow is a Sunday and you could
rest all day in the house, or whatever you so desire. . . ."

Turner left Andy and turned about to hear
what Rudds was saying, and Giles and Imogene
went forward to stand before him. There were
whispered agreements, frankly spoken, and the
bargain was made. Turner said that he would perform the ceremony for the money Wilson had at
hand, that this was sufficient, and the license was
offered for inspection. The people settled into a
pleased silence. When Andy was released he stood
back near the farther door, and he straightened
his back against the wall and quieted his shaking
legs by standing on first one of them and then the
other. Bending in a slow rhythm and beating to
and fro, his head shaking unevenly, he went out
through the door, as if the throb of the singing
were still beating upon him. Philly knew that he
had scarcely understood what had released him,
that he would stand beyond the kitchen door or

hobble up and down on the path to the garden, and later he would draw himself a cool fresh bucket of water from the well, and he would say, "God be praised!" over and over in a stiff whisper. Now the words of the marriage went forward and the quiet held, the words uniting Imogene and Giles running solemnly through the settled hush.

The house-painters left as soon as the last words were said and several others followed them. The men who sat near the door came forward, with Callie and Rudds and the young girls, to shake Imogene and Giles by the hand, to wish them good luck. Words expressing pleasure and surprise were passed swiftly about. Hester Trigg came to the fore, making some pleasant speech, her moist mouth spread wide to laugh at her joke, as if she had helped bring the wedding about. Her hearty presence, standing before Giles and Imogene, gave approval and added to Philly's security. Philly felt a mass of pleasure arise in her breast to spread to her shoulders and overflow in her throat. She saw that all the young boys and girls were startled and that the women were pleased, and that the men were not angry, although some of them were indifferent and made ready to go home without comment. She knew that Andy would not come back until the guests had left. "I always told you Philly loved a wedden," they were saying as they passed toward the door.

"It's a pity Mr. Andy got so upset and all, he couldn't stay to see."

They were out at the doorstep and in the yard, talking. Philly left the hearth to its own security and stood beside the door to wish the guests good-bye. All the young girls and boys went across the pasture with Giles and Imogene to conduct them, all singing and teasing, on the way home.

IV

OUTSIDE BLAIR'S HOUSE THE NOISE SPREAD AND FLAT-
tened against the large old trees. The hound rolled
out a long howl from somewhere beyond the barn
and the burst of high tones under the low moan-
ing was answered far away by some other dog that
barked at a farmhouse off to the west. They
answered each other, back and forth, across the
swell and roll of the land. While the people were
coming out of the house, while they lingered over
their good-byes and made pleasant sayings and
banter, expressing surprise and delight, Ben Shepherd walked near Bonnie White, for he shrank
from the intimacy with Wilson into which he had
entered before the wedding. The people were
turning here and there, some of them leaving in
vehicles. All the young people, with Rudds and

his wife, kept close to Giles and Imogene, as if they meant to follow wherever these two went. There was laughter and teasing, and presently all were in the pasture back of the house, for the married pair had tried to slip apart and take a short path homeward. They were walking over Blair's pasture, the way leading toward the creek and toward the place where Ben had formerly camped.

The boys, with Rudds, had been whispering and some plan was under way. The moon was well toward the west, becoming a great red ball as it sank, and the light it shed was a vast dim glow, diffused and strange. The girls asked continual questions. Their fluttering voices tossed about and they surrounded Giles and Imogene, being more noisy and frolicsome than the boys, who were secretly planning.

"When, Imogene, did you ever think to marry in Miss Philly's house?"

"Who thought it out? Did you, or did Miss Philly?"

"I'm surprised old Mr. Andy ever thought to make up a wedden."

"Old Mr. Andy! Whoever would 'a' thought it!"

"I didn't suppose old Mr. Andy cared whe'r anybody got married or not."

"I'm surprised all over. I'm all in a twitchet."

"I'm in such a twitchet I can hardly stand on my two feet." This last was spoken by Effie Trigg. Her voice was fluttering out of her shaking mouth and she bobbed about among the other girls. She tried to keep the place nearest to Imogene, but a thin girl pushed nearer and cried out:

"Tell me this, Imogene. Did you have it in mind all day today while you worked at home?"

"Don't say work to Imogene. Let Imogene forget work for a spell," Rudds's wife speaking. She kept near to Imogene as if she would help her, knowing that mischief was afoot.

The boys came back and all were walking slowly over the pasture, the boys and the girls together, and it seemed then as if the boys had given up their plan. While they were still the strange midnight settled about them. The shadows were long diffused shapes that stretched eastward because the moon was falling away toward the west. The nightjars were flying in the air overhead, making long sweeping and gliding curves upward and about, crying "Peent." Ben knew that the boys had not given up their plan, that they had but satisfied themselves with arranging it, that they had come back to begin to bring it about.

"How'll he get over the creek?" a girl asked.

"At the watergap."

"A big rain up above today. The creek is like a river."

"He's bound to cross at the watergap."

"He's bound to go by the watergap."

The boys were pulling and plucking at Giles, holding him back, dividing him from Imogene. Another would take her arm and walk away with her. The boys who had gone ahead had fastened the gate with a wire, and the bride was obliged to climb over. The girls gathered about her again, asking their questions, and when the gate was passed the boys went ahead toward the watergap, and Ben knew that there was trouble prepared there. He kept near Bonnie, feeling in her some security, as if she would interpret all that happened for him, as if she would explain and temper Giles and Imogene for him and make known what the boys had in mind. Robbie May had refused to dance with him at the party. Each time he had asked her she had tossed her head and taken the arm of another. It seemed now as if goodness had settled upon Bonnie, as if she had the largest measure of it that the world held.

A great rain had fallen high up in the head-waters of the creek. The rush and roar of the water was heard up in the pasture, and the yellow flood,

stained with the topsoil from the plowed cornfields and the newly set tobacco would churn and
rush and roar about the palings of the watergap
where the fence crossed the stream. The low
stringers at the top of the structure would make a
narrow foothold. Ben had seen the rain clouds
shifting far to the east during the early afternoon,
and here was the roaring, flowing mass of it gathered to be a torrent that surged down between
the hills. The night was clear, every cloud being
gone. A sudden warm breeze would strike the face
now and then, one blown from some sunny midday field, or again a cool waft would float up from
the creek laden with the odor of the silt and the
water. Knowing this of the air, of the moisture,
the stream, the far reach of the hills, Ben felt momentarily as if he knew less of the people who were
turning and chattering all about and knew less of
Giles and Imogene, as if he knew more of flood
and fire than he did of what went forward within
these men and girls. The girls were pushing and
bantering, clinging to Imogene, but some of the
young men had gone forward toward the creek.

All at once, trying to become a part with the
crying throng that turned and jerked and whistled
and called about Giles and Imogene, trying to say
something such as they might say, Ben shouted:

"It's my belief there was something under the hearth. Something hidden."

"What hidden?" several voices cried out.

"Hidden what?"

"Who hidden?"

"What for?"

"Hidden what for?"

The words lay against the waning moonlight, said now, but disregarded. They were racing over the second pasture and down through the tree-grown slope, toward the creek.

The young men had planned to carry Giles away and lock him into Rudds's barn. There was to be some difficulty at the watergap and afterward they were to tie Giles, hands and feet, with ropes or wires, and carry him away. Some of the roisterers had rushed ahead to find the bindings and to lie in wait at the watergap. Giles would be obliged to cross here or wade in water above the knees. The girls did not know clearly what was going forward but some hint of mischief was whispered about. In the glade the trees were loosely scattered and the brush was left here and there, after an uneven clearing. The moonlight was waning and thus the glade was dimly lit by a faint

gray light so that shapes were seen, but it became
more and more difficult to discern one from another unless voices spoke. Some of the girls called
Rudds's wife "Aunt Ronnie" or "Cousin Ronnie."
She followed Imogene with much difficulty, struggling with the briars and panting at the steep
places, but she kept near at hand.

"Those boys have got a blight," she said.

The girls said but little but they were in a mood
to help Imogene and Giles escape from their tor-
mentors and to save Imogene from further hard-
ships. "Help get her off," they said, their voices
fluttering in half-whispers. "Get ahead of the
boys. . . ."

"A blight on themselves, seems," the aunt Ronnie said. "First it's try to make a bet there's something under Philly's floor, and now make trouble
for Imogene. As if Philly and Imogene hadn't
seen enough trouble already. Those boys have got
a blight. They take all the pretty part outen a
wedden."

"Boys will be boys," Rudds said. "Boys will . . ."

"Boys will be boys, yes, but you, Lester Rudds,
had a heap to do to help-out and make these boys
be boys. You're a good hand to show boys how to
be boys. For an old man you're a sight."

Ben followed Bonnie, keeping near her when

she moved about among the other girls. "Why wouldn't Robbie May dance with me?" he asked her.

"I don't know for sure," she answered. "I don't know, but I've got a little idea why 'twas."

"Why?"

"I'll tell you my idea, but you must never breathe it to a soul that I told you. You must cross your heart and body."

Ben agreed to pledge himself thus.

"Cross your heart and body and hope you may die if ever you tell," she said earnestly. She was in no bantering mood, but spoke almost fearfully.

"I'll do it. I'll do all you say. I hope I may die . . ."

"I don't know for sure, but I think it was because she saw you once in the graveyard. In the Shepherd burying-place."

"I had a right to be there," Ben said slowly. "I was in my rights. You mean I saw her, is what you mean. I'm sorry though."

"She holds it against you, maybe."

The girls were scattering here and there, shouting and struggling with the uneven path. All the young men were running down toward the water-gap, which was not far away now.

"Go, now, quick!" the aunt Ronnie said to

Giles and Imogene. "Off that way. Go. Don't even stop to look back."

The girls were scattering in every direction and gathering together again, darting in and out among the bushes and the little haw trees. Two of the boys were coming back from the creek hollow, pretending that they had come back to help the girls descend, and the girls made a great ado over the steep decline.

"Where are they?" Sims called out from below.

"Here they are!" there was shouting, up and down the glade. "Here they are, here!"

"Giles, where's he?"

"He's here!"

"Here we are!"

"Where?"

"Here!"

"No, here!"

The girls had a great difficulty with the briars and the stones, with a fallen wire, with Effie Trigg who had to be helped down continually and with Robbie May who was particular as to who should help her. They went in and out among the bushes, making a delay. They started a song and stopped to finish it. The young men seemed intent upon the girls, as if they had wandered aimlessly from their plan, but Ben knew that when the time came to fulfill it they were prepared at the water-gap.

At the creek there was a gathering of the throng and very much laughter. It was the opinion of the men that Giles would be obliged to cross here since the stream was high. One tested the depth with a long pole and found it to be about three feet. They said that Giles would be obliged to come, sooner or later, and they waited, keeping very quiet. When they had waited twenty minutes or more some of the men went back to search the woods and the fields, but Giles and Imogene were not found.

"God's sake!" one cried out. "God's own sake!"

"God's own sake and then some!"

"That's what I say. He must 'a' swum over."

"Love o' God, he must, surely!"

"Swum over and carried Imogene on his back."

"He's not this side. He must be on t'other. I looked under every bush this-side Blair's and he's not there."

"Listen, there he is now."

"Hit's only a scrooch-owl. Giles is no scrooch-owl."

"Waded over, I reckon, waist high, and carried Imogene."

They made many opinions, restating their wonder. When Bonnie's young man came to claim her, the plan to kidnap Giles having failed, Ben went from the throng which was slowly dispersing. He heard the Rudds group, with the girls and their young men, going up the field on the opposite side of the creek toward Rudds's home, and a few of the young men went back on the way that they had come. At Stoner's place he mounted the back stairway to the room used by the hired men and he found his bed. There were two other beds in the room and in these Larkin and Grove were sleeping.

On Sunday morning a Sabbath quiet and rest lay over the farms. Waking in the upper back room, hearing no farm bells ring, Ben's first thought was of Imogene. He knew that he would be expected to help with the work of the barns, to feed the horses and the mules, and that he should arise when he heard Stoner walking below. Imogene had a continual part in his drowsy waking, at first as a pleasant shape in which any content one might prefer could be discerned. While she had stood up to be married she had been a tall girl with a few wrinkles on the instep of one of her stockings. He thought of her in Giles Wilson's kitchen making a breakfast, wearing the dress she had worn at the party because she could as yet have no other. He conjectured and contrived for her, turning the thought of her about: Perhaps she had been muddied going over the creek. Perhaps she had slept rolled in a sheet, having no night-clothes with her. Now, in the morning, Giles would be taking her out to show her his barn and the chicken-houses and she would be carrying out the hens their curds.

Ben heard Stoner walking on the porch below and he found that he had been dreaming. He arose drowsily, leaving Larkin and Grove asleep in their beds, and he went down to perform his morning tasks.

Giving the mules their corn or helping Stoner with the cow, he returned again and again to Imogene. She was in and out of his mind, as a picture, as a shape, a desire, a fear, a dim recollection, as two lines out of a ballad:

> A chieftain to the Highlands bound,
> Cries, "Boatman, do not tarry . . ."

She had come into the party as a tall girl with a plump, pale face. She had seemed as of little account as she stood behind the other girls who were dancing. Then she was near the mantel, unimportant, pale, her voice never heard. But suddenly she came to the fore as the one Giles was about to marry and the whole throng was still in her behalf, as still as she had been. She was of sufficient weight to quiet all the noises and to force the evangelist to leave off his threats. She was then a tall woman, her face moist and her eyes frightened, her manner straightforward, shy but determined. She was looking into the face of the minister. When the hard voice said, "Man and wife," she turned slightly about, as if she would leave at once, but several were shaking her hands and one or two kissed her. She seemed powerful out in the pasture, everybody pressing near to hear, wanting to be touching her. She was moist and soft and fearful, everybody wanting to be near and wanting to be a part with her in all that went forward.

She was going over the pasture beside Giles or was plucked away from Giles for the moment. She was panting from a struggle at the gate. She was climbing over the gate, helped over by Sims and another who had pushed Giles away. Down the second pasture and into the glade where the light was dim. The threat of the watergap lay ahead. She was tired and was stopping to rest, catching her breath. The girls were darting about in the brush. Imogene was more than they, being con-

tinually in the mind of everyone. She was soft and
moist and warm, shy but forward-going, afraid and
yielding everywhere, but determined, slipping unevenly and uneasily down the path. Once Sims had
her and was taking her away to the right. Then
she was melting away into the dark of the trees
toward the left, gone more in Bonnie's whisper,
"They're gone," than in any visible departure.
She and Giles were off somewhere among the trees,
running farther. Somewhere off, far to the left,
Giles had carried her over the creek. Giles would
have a great delight in having out-done Sims, but
he would be cautious and fearful until he had left
the creek behind. They would creep along fencerows, keeping themselves low in the hollows. Beyond Rudds's land Giles would come to his own
field. She seemed to be gone far then, and Ben
returned to a diffused thought of her in the parlor
and in the pasture, beside the mantel and climbing over the gate.

Larkin and Grove came down the stairs and
went away, saying that they were going to the
creek to fish. After Ben had eaten breakfast he
heard the church bells ringing and they were not
unlike the farm bells of the weekdays. A high,
thin, impatient jingle, asking something, appeal-
ing anxiously, came first; but later two bells rang

at the same time, the high-pitched unevenness beating and tinkling over and about a slow, determined throb that seemed nearer at hand, as if it were from the church in the village.

Thinking out a sequence for Imogene while he made his clothing neat, Ben had deeply within a constant resentment which was directed toward the Rudds girl, Robbie May. He thought that he would show her his scorn in some way if he should see her again. He wished in some way to rise above her and to show her that he cared in no way whether she came or went. He wanted more than anything else to forget her, and he wished that he might forget her name. After the church bells had throbbed and tinkled together, while he walked from the house to wait for the farmer under the trees of the lawn he thought that he might send Robbie May the bone of his ancestor, the relic which he carried in his pocket.

Many of the people gathered at the two churches, one of them in the village and the other beyond, but at noon they dispersed to slip quickly back through the roadways and spread to the farm-houses where they sat to rest under the trees. Ben went to church with Stoner and Mrs. Stoner, driv-

ing in a respectable car that had been used for
several years. The preacher gave an impassioned
account of Sodom, of Lot and his wife, and the
pillar of salt. He leaned over the assembled gathering of farmers and cried out for the hardness of
basalt and the lean, impenetrable stiffness and
lack-savor of those who turn back toward the cities
where wickedness is common and carelessness the
rule of life. The pillar and Lot seemed far from
these people now at the season of the harvest. The
men and women sat relaxed, half dreaming, and it
seemed to Ben that thus the passion of the minister, since it touched them nowhere, rested them as
they viewed it from afar.

After noon had passed, Stoner sat under the
trees not far from the place where Ben had painted
the shutters, and he talked of what he had heard of
the earlier Shepherds and of what he remembered.
He was eager to tell.

"You're kin of mine," he said. "You're kin to
Imogene Cundy on her mother's side, and kin to
Philly Blair too, and all the Rudds lot this side of
old Dick—up in the graveyard—and kin to Giles
Wilson in another way around, but it's all a long
way off."

He began to tell of Richard, Ben's grandfather,
and of the farm toward Wilson's place where Rich-

ard used to live. There had been at one time a
house near the burying-ground but it had burned
one cold night in a winter which was not now
clearly remembered or divided from many other
winters. The foundation could still be seen over
beyond the graveyard, among the briars. Ben had
not found it, he said, not knowing that there had
been such a house, but when he had stated this he
began to feel that it was untrue, that he should
have known or that he had somehow heard of the
older house. It had been the first home of the
Shepherds, built by Tobias himself, but as Stoner
remembered it, recalling more and more as he
turned the matter about in mind, it had been the
home of Joel. As Stoner talked of this marrying
and that grandmother, Ben saw that he was related by distant blood ties to nearly all the people
of the whole community.

"It was said old Joel's father was born in the
fort. John, his name was. And that puts it back to
his father, Tobias, and the originals."

While the voice droned thus, naming ancient
persons, Ben thought fitfully of the bone which he
carried in his pocket and he wished that he might
know from whom it was derived. He asked then
about the graves, trying to identify them, thinking
of Robbie May and holding a deep-seated distaste

for her scornful way of being as it was directed toward himself. Stoner thought that the grave deep within the thicket, where nobody ever went, must have been the grave of old Tobias himself.

"It ought to be marked again," he said. "I must go up there after harvest and get things in better shape."

"It ought to be covered over," Ben said. "It's in a manner open. You'd be surprised to see what's there. . . ."

A slight distaste passed over him, a faint and unexpressed nausea—Robbie May catching the arm of another and moving off in a dance. She had been gay and bright at the party, a trifle silly, he thought. Away from the horse she seemed more quick, but she was not less proud. He remembered the figure in the flowered dress running down from the hill, and before that scene the voice calling out, "It's nine!" At the party she had been all of these two former appearances and something more. Her proud manner defended her from the results of her headlong decisions. She was in no way like Imogene although, like Imogene, she had a forbidden lover. Whatever might be the outcome of her secret trysts, the whole community would not be shaken for her as it had been for the other girl. Old ladies would say of her, "It serves her right . . ." or they would click their tongues. They would say, "I just expected it." She would have to look out for herself and that was the reason she rode proudly on her horse. No doubt she had always been riding. At the party her eyes were bright and angry, as if they had shut their secrets within, as if she dared Ben to know what he had seen and dared him to remember.

"Sam Cundy, he'll about burn Philly's house down," Mrs. Stoner said, thinking they were talking of Imogene. "I wouldn't be surprised . . ."

"Looks like the whole country is in a sweat over what happened there last night," Stoner said to Ben. "But nobody but Cundy is sorry."

"I wouldn't be surprised," Mrs. Stoner called out. "But he'll get over it. He'll about eat his Christmas dinner with Imogene and be jolly a-plenty. But they say he's a mad old hornet now."

Cundy had gone into a rage when he heard that Imogene had left his home. Early Sunday morning he had torn her dresses down off the closet hooks and burned them in the kitchen fire. He had gone back to her room three times to find something more to mutilate and destroy. One of the Cundy boys had told Stoner of this anger while the men waited outside the church during the morning. Mrs. Stoner always heard what her husband said when he spoke directly to her, as if she heard him without the use of her ears.

"He said the third time Cundy carried down Imogene's schoolbooks and burned them, put them in the fire. Like he'd be glad to make away with what she used to be and all that ever she was." Mrs. Stoner spoke, looking at her husband's mouth, waiting for his reply.

"You couldn't say it's the Shepherd blood in Cundy, makes him do it?" Ben asked.

"No. He's got a sprinkle of Shepherd blood too. But it's not blood makes him do it. It's some other. What is it makes Cundy do it, Mammy?" he asked his wife.

"It's devilment. It's what he holds in head and can't forget. It's what he thinks about his own self. It's pride. . . . He can't see it any way but his own way. He's like old Joel Shepherd, only different. He's too young a man to have the devilment take a-hold of him though. . . . He can't bear to have his household changed in the way it goes. . . . He has got the habit of haven Imogene always in the house so he can run in and tell her if anything goes wrong. While he tells her he thinks up a way to cure what's amiss. He uses her that way, in place of Lispy. Then he says she can't go and he's always in a habit to have his youngones mind every word he speaks. Imogene is the one he needs most and she breaks away. Then his devilment boils over and he tears her clothes down off the hooks and puts her, in a manner, inside the fire. It's devilment."

They had said it was not blood that made Cundy rage thus, but some other, some active substance, "devilment." Stoner pursed his lips together and considered this opinion, and Mrs. Stoner watched his face, knowing what he was thinking. Ben left them consorting thus together and floated, mentally, about his own affairs. He had decided fully that he would send the bone to Robbie May. If his mere presence at the party had reminded her unpleasantly that she had been seen in the graveyard, he would, he determined, send her some real reminder, some real token of the place. He would wrap the relic in a piece of neat paper and fit it into a little box. He would ask Mrs. Stoner for a little pasteboard container, for a little wooden box, if she had one, and he would address a note to Robbie May. Stoner had left the matter of Cundy's anger and was telling now in what way he himself belonged to the old race of Shepherds. Ben listened now, going back to Kitty who spelled the name She-pard, and while Stoner talked, making lines and signs in the air, Ben thought of the wide-reaching branches of the race families as they were spread out in the charts in books, and he went back to the ants, thinking that their galleries underground were like the spreading and dividing lines on the charts. In the books would be the royal families, the kings and their offspring, arranged as a stiff inverted tree, the branches running downward on the paper to make more and more branching twigs, like the ants, and in the end of each one would be an egg or a pupa case. When he thought of the pupa case he wanted to let spittle fly, to spew them all out of his mouth. Leaning over, looking into the grass while Stoner talked and seeing what went on there, he wondered if all of them, even the tumblebugs, could be serious about what they did when they prepared their eggs for hatching. The tumblebugs were the curious ha-ha of nature. In them the world met itself coming back from somewhere, from its own glory, or whatnot. He was lost in his own thinking, drowned in the somewhere of his devising, and he began to compose his note to Robbie May, saying: "You have got a proud back and a pretty face. The tumblebugs have got proud backs too, if you have ever noticed them at work over their egg baskets."

"I wouldn't be surprised, though, if he didn't

make trouble for Philly," Mrs. Stoner said, weary of her husband's recital. "I wouldn't wonder if I heard he'd been there."

Her voice made an alteration in Ben's mood and he shifted and probed at the wording of the note, repeating it. It seemed to him then that the reference to the tumblebugs would put him in a class with Cundy, as if it would needlessly mutilate some of the prettier part of life. He made the note short and let it turn upon the bone. "You have got a proud back and a pretty face. Mr. Stoner says you are my cousin ten steps removed or more. You do not want to dance with a wraith now, but some day you may need to. I recommend on that day this bone."

Mrs. Stoner brought a few tart yellow apples from the orchard, the first of the season. Several neighbors came, and after they were seated some of the apples were eaten. It was a matter for wonder and delight that the apples had ripened before the oat harvest. One of the visitors called Mrs. Stoner "Cousin Verdie," but the other, an older woman, called her "Verdie" without a title. This one was more deaf than Mrs. Stoner, and there was frequent shouting back and forth. The visitors gave much praise for the apples.

"I make a big show with a few," Mrs. Stoner said. "I say I make a big show with only a few."

The apples made Stoner remember more to tell. He had filched apples from the great orchard that used to grow back of the old Shepherd house. Once old Shepherd had fired a shotgun when the boys were stealing in the orchard.

"Maybe the old man never meant more than to scare us. He was, I recollect, a tall old man, bent half double." There was more of the apples, the voice droning forward. An angry, wounded old man, almost spent of life, creeping about as if he were housed under his large bent back, looking out from faded gray eyes, he walked about among the tall bushes of his great unkempt orchard. Ben's thought made quick excursions away from the path of this discourse or returned to wander slowly beside it. One generation of the old race had written the name Shepard. They made, all together, a long thread of life, reaching from the birth in the fort downward. The succession of grandfathers spread back and forth through time, they being old flesh, knotted, bone-infested, hard, crooked, and dried out. It was difficult to think of them as having been at any time small and new-born, fresh and young and increasing. They were going, withering, becoming less, and they turned

—a complete succession—into random bones, into branching, stony spines of one calcareous matter. Tobias, John, Joel, John B., Richard, and farther —this was the sequence of the succession, and the first was as dry as the last, as spent, as knotted and marred. Richard, John B., Joel, John, and Tobias —all one in departure. They had been five and they had differed one from the others, one being old when another was young. This was dry, quiet, passive, Sabbath thinking. They, these bony creatures, made with their succession time itself; they made a century among them.

The passive, Sunday trend of thought continued, running beside Stoner's recital. Somewhere in the long line thus stretched through time a kettle of gold had been put into the hills, in the middle of them, no doubt, as if one tied a knot in a thread to say "here," to say "at this point." While Stoner talked, his mouth made sequences of shapes as if it were saying, "Argolis, Laconia, Attica"; as if "hortor, hortaris." Ben had a sudden flash of life spring within him, as though in Imogene he were living again. There was a pleasure in her, the country was torn apart for her, the people were disturbed for her, heightened to a newer fervor. In her the boys and the men were more of themselves, more lustful and hearty and cruel. The girls were careful and cunning, preserving her and her way of life. He brought an end to the long recital when he stood up in the grass and stretched his arms, flinging up his head.

A man came riding at a sharp walk, coming from the north and passing along the road toward the village. He rode evenly, as if he were set forward on a purpose, but when he saw the company on Stoner's lawn he checked his horse and dismounted, hitching the horse, a tall roan, near the gate. He walked into the lawn and forthwith a hush settled over the gathering there. "Here he is, now. . . . Look, here . . ." several murmured, and they moved back, making space. Stoner brought the new-comer a chair and a pitcher of water, and someone spoke, as if he would like to begin comment on the state of the harvest. Ben knew that the man was Cundy although none had called his name. He seemed short of breath as if he were wearied or angered. He wore a clean blue cotton shirt and trousers of the same cloth, and a coat from some dark woolen suit. When he stood he seemed very large and tall, and when he sat in the chair Stoner offered he still dominated the gathering, sitting forward uneasily, about to rise.

"The head is right pretty this time," Stoner said, speaking of the wheat. "I look for a good yield."

"Wheat is a sight better this time than last," another spoke, and then another:

"Wheat are better'n the oats, but the oats are not far behind neither. . . ."

"Rudds has got a field that'll bring all of sixty bushels to the acre. By golly! I never saw such a head."

"Talk about Imogene," Cundy burst out, his hand lifted and his face swelling and growing red. "Whyn't you talk Imogene? That's what you want. Talk Imogene and Giles Wilson. Imogene Cundy is her name. Cundy. Born a Cundy and a Cundy she is to this God's day. . . ."

"I wouldn't want to say a word against Imogene. Everybody thinks fair of Imogene in all the country. She's a fine lady." Stoner said aloud what others were murmuring. "Nobody could damage Imogene in our sight. It's like I said yesterday . . ."

"She's a hussy," Cundy roared out. "I reckon I know."

There was a period of quiet, nobody offering to enter into conflict with Cundy's anger. Finally a man said, speaking quietly:

"She's a good modest girl. I always said, minds her own business."

"Minds her business and asks mighty little for herself in life, I always thought. . . ."

"She's what I said. I'll prove it!"

"I reckon I'd better go on home now," one said, and another rose also. "By the time I get there sundown will be close at hand. . . . I think I'll leave you. . . . Much obliged, Bud Stoner, for a pleasant afternoon." One or two left uneasily, trying to make the departure easy and natural.

"She's a hussy," Cundy roared out. He stood up to talk, his hand lifted higher. "I know what I say. In four days' time I'll prove what I've got in mind. Let her go now. Let her think she's safe for a spell. I'll prove what I say. She's not fitten to sit in the house with a man's wife. She's what I say."

"Let him go," they whispered. They were stirring about; they were figures moving here and there in a senseless play. Cundy had moved off as if he would leave. "Don't say 'sit awhile longer,' but let him go wherever he's a mind to. . . ." They were hard shapes moving roughly about, undetermined where they were bound, whispering, "Let him go on. . . ." Let him go forever. They would be turning about in the same dance to the end of the earth. A bone rubbing upon a bone. A bone hurting a bone, wanting a bone, shapes filched out of the clods and set up in life. Those wanting departure seemed scarcely able to go, but they turned about lingering, wanting to outstay the last that had come. The senseless sunshine slanted under the trees where Ben had painted, and the hard light lay over the front of the house. The senseless cloth of their garments stood up before the trees and their nakedness itself was clothing that hid only a little of their inner uselessness. They were sad and awkward, trying to be kind. They were leaving then, one saying, "It won't be me," and another, "I got work to do in another quarter. . . ." Cundy went back along the way he had come. None wanted to ride with him. Mrs. Stoner and her friend, the deaf woman called Julie, were left sitting apart.

Ben went away to help Stoner with the work of the barn. In a little while he came back across the stepping stones from the barnyard and waited uncertainly about. There seemed nothing left to do. The day was nearly over and the twilight at hand. Mrs. Stoner and the other woman were still sitting on the lawn. They were leaning together to shout.

"I wouldn't want to be down in that sink where Giles Wilson put his pappy."

"What say, Julie?"

"I say I wouldn't want to be buried down in that-there sink where Giles put his pa."

"You what, Julie?"

"I say Tom's grave's down off the hill from where my lot is."

"Tom did what, Julie?"

"I say Tom's lot's down off the hill from where mine is."

"What say?"

"I say Tom's buried down off the hill from where I am . . . down . . . down off the hill, in the sink. . . . I say buried down off the hill from where I am. . . ."

The other one had heard at last. "You're not buried there yet?" she asked.

"What say, Verdie?"

"I say you ain't buried there yet, are you?"

"What say?"

"I say you are not buried there, buried yet, are you?"

"Well, no, I reckon I ain't."

They were quiet for a short space before they took up another matter, beating and harrowing through it to a final agreement, gathering sense out of their phrases by minute particles, patiently pieced together.

Although the two painters slept in the room with Ben, occupying two other small beds, he heard them talking together but little. Larkin slept nervously, turning about much during the night, and often he mumbled in his dreams. Grove lay heavily drugged, as a great beast fitted unevenly into the small bed where he seemed out of place, as if the bed might fall away from under him at any moment. Larkin was careful of his attire, and he laid his paint-soiled garments in an orderly arrangement on his chair each night. Grove dropped his at the side of his bed and laid himself down heavily, cursing the farmer's wife. On Monday Mrs. Stoner offered Ben a room at the front of the house, but he told her that he would stay where he had been.

"I didn't know when you came here that you would be kinfolks. I didn't know you'd be one of the Shepherds," she said.

He asked her for a little wooden box, saying that he wished to send something by the mail. She was pleased that he asked this favor of her since he had refused the favor of the forward part of the house, and she went to the pantry where she found a little wooden box with a sliding top. Ben hid the little box in his pocket until he was alone in the field and then, fitting the bone into it, he found that it would serve well. The bone and the box and his own intentions seemed to fit well together, and the satisfaction in finding a suitable container for the relic filled him with a sort of pleasure, so that he felt a vague indifference of Robbie May, as if he had already worked free of her.

The tassels of the wheat stood up tall and yellow, daintily sprangled in the sunlight, a quivering lace that was made at each moment and destroyed as the light changed and the wind blew over it, an endless infinite lace running outward with the sweep of the field. The rye, taller than the wheat and lighter at the head, tossed more freely in the summer winds so that waves went over it as if it were the surface of a sea. The bluegrass was past the flower, in the seed, and the farmers were stripping it here and there for seed grass. Ben helped Stoner at this task, swinging a hand stripper that reached long inflexible fingers of wood into the high grain and came away with small ripening pods that held the seeds. Sappy and tender, this substance in a heap made a soft froth that was like feathers as it was piled in a basket. While Ben worked thus gathering grass seed from strips of unpastured fencerows and grass lots, the two thieves worked indoors, treating the inside woodwork of the house with a coat of white paint.

When they had finished the inside they would apply another coat of the paint to the outside, and thus Ben thought that they might outstay him in the community, for he knew that he would have a message in a few days telling him to come home, reminding him that he had overstayed his time.

The land waited two days or three for the first harvest, seeming ready. But the men held it to a finer readiness and required these few hours of waiting. Then beyond the creek, toward the north and west from Stoner's farm, Rudds began to cut the grain. The slow-moving procession—men and beasts and cutting machine—went in a crooked square about the field to change it from a rolling, upward-tilted swell of yellow grass to a flattened stubble floor on which arose evenly the gathered shocks.

"I didn't want to leave my comrades," Ben said, still addressing Mrs. Stoner in his thought. "I say, I wanted to keep an eye on my roommates," he said, swinging the stripper to get the seed from the grass.

The week was mounting toward a climax with the swift changes that were coming to the grain fields as they turned to a riper yellow, as they swayed a few hours thus in the sun, and were entered by the harvesters and cut, laid out in long squares and rectangles of shocks beside straight walls of the standing grain, as the labor went forward. On Thursday Ed Sims drove the reaper through Stoner's field. Stoner himself sat high on the implement, above the cutting knives and the long sweep, to swing the lever and throw off the bundles when they were tied by the machine and passed outward. Ben gathered the spilled bundles and stacked them in shocks.

Sims took the heat of the sun into his body, being ruddy and brown of it, as if he might hold more continually. His large arms were bare, the sleeves of his shirt torn out at the shoulders. He talked only a little as the reaper went around the field, but his being was continually talkative, and it seemed that he might at any moment burst into ready speech or singing. He kept a great good humor.

Ben walked back and forth across the field, setting the thrown bundles into shocks that made the field teem, for it had arisen to lift its plenty high up toward the sun while the cutting lasted. A throng of powers and persons were in the field. Ed Sims, in his fine good humor, as if he might at any moment leap again into some rude song, rode first on the strongest mule to guide the cutting tool through the grain. Stoner, sitting high on the machine, was cautious of the sun and was ready, if he felt a touch of it, to call his black laborer from plowing the corn and bid him take the place on the top of the reaper. There were the four horses that stepped evenly over the level places but tugged as they were driven where the path led upward with the swell of the hill. Ben himself, then, making shocks, and over these the waves of heat that beat downward from the sun, the heat that arose reflected from the ground, the grasshoppers and gallinippers that spread off before the cutting and leaped away over the stubble. Once, passing near Sims, while he turned the horses at a corner, delayed in turning, Ben asked if he had known Imogene long.

"Lord, yes, I knew her."

Ben had wanted to ask of the other one, Robbie May, but he wanted better not to know anything of her and to undo all that he already had of her, and so he let his asking stay with the calling of Imogene's name.

Turning about the field, picking up the sheaves as the reaper dropped them, Ben heard these words, holding them above the clicking of the knives while the mower went twice around the swath. Sims rode easily on the lead horse. He was good-natured and profane, slightly obscene, innocent and direct and lewd, and there was nothing between him and the ground, nothing between him and the sun, as if in him they made a hearty flower. When he had gone twice around the field, up the long rise by the eastern boundary and down on the other side, and back, again and again, he spoke, flinging out a farther comment:

"There's few in this whole ding-busted country I don't know."

He rode off along the wall of the wheat and the roar of the machine was like a wind and the tinkle of the cutting was like a high, sharp music. When he came opposite Ben again there was no need for turning, and he went steadily forward, making sheaves, the four large mules trampling through the stubble. He shouted to Ben, his voice lifting above the sweep and the high jingle of the knives.

"Especially the women-folks."

He was gone slowly down the path made by the mower. His skin glistened in the sun, being red with the heat and moist with sweat. He bestrode the largest beast of the four and he held all by the reins that were skillfully lifted or drawn or turned in his hand. He matched the reaper exactly to the uncut wall each time and held a true course down the length of the field, riding easily. "I know all of 'em," he said, passing Ben again.

The farther hills and the fields toward the west, toward Blair's and Rudds's farmsteads, seemed faintly lavender under the high light of the sun. Gallinippers and grasshoppers, walking-sticks and walking-leaves, bumblebees and wasps and crickets, tossed about and went in and out of the high grain, or they found new hiding when the knives left the stubble unshaded and wide to the sun. Sims rode into this tossing and splattering life, coming up from the farther side of the field, shouting:

"I don't know any harm about her, either." Turning the horses to fit the reaper again to the wheat, "I don't know e'er a word of harm about Imogene."

Ben stacked the bundles so that the shock would resist a shower if one fell, and he was helped by a black man who worked in the lower side of the field. Through one corner of the field a gathering of ants was moving through the soft soil and between the stalks of the left stubble. At the edge of the field they were coming out of a crevice in the loam and running forward toward some place Ben had not discovered, carrying young ants that were wrapped in the white pupa cases. Ben stacked the shocks in regular rows, setting one down in the middle of the ants' theater of action because the order of the field required that one should come at that place, and he saw that his feet caused a great havoc among the ants. He turned neither to the right to save nor to the left to destroy, but went forward over them as a mindless fate that followed the bent of the field. Leaning forward to see what happened he set a measured stride upon the ants, neither longer nor shorter than was his habit, and he traced their fate back to the nature of his habitual stride, which was such as it was because he had the bones of the Shepherds under his muscles, they being of such and such a length. "Thus do the bones of the Shepherds become, for a little while, the destiny of the ants," he said, walking evenly forward, neither pity nor wrath in his mind.

Toward noon a rider came along the road, riding slowly and aimlessly, as if he were uncertain whether to stop or to continue on his way. Ben forgot the rider when his work took him to the slope farther from the highroad, but when he came to the top of the field again he saw that someone had come through the gate from the meadow that lay beside the road and that he was now riding across the stubble. Sims, cursing, worked steadily forward, as if he would make a protest toward the new-comer, as if he would gladly mow him down with the wheat if he stood near to it, and he swept the work past the rider and out toward the farther reach of the cutting. But here the farm bell sounded over the fields to call the men home for dinner, a flat metallic gonging from the tall bell beside the kitchen porch. Stoner called out that it was time the work stopped now, and Sims left the saddle of the lead horse and began to help Ben release the teams.

"It's a fine day to make a harvest," Stoner said to Cundy. "I reckon you're ready to cut at your place too."

"I aim for the boys to begin to cut tomorrow," Cundy answered. "They know their business without me to tend after them. A man's daughter gone astray and it's not likely he'll keep his mind long on a wheat harvest."

"I reckon she's not gone very far astray," Stoner called out. "If we never go any further we'll keep a straight road to heaven, Sam."

"She's gone to the devil. She's a hussy. She's not fitten to sit down in a man's house. . . ."

He seemed about to burst with his wrath and he wheeled his tall horse about, facing Stoner. Ben released the mules from the chains and straps that held them to the mower, and he took two of them, leaving Sims and Stoner one each so that they might ride across to the barn. Stoner mounted his horse but he stayed to answer Cundy, and a few swift words passed back and forth. "I can prove what I say," Cundy would cry out, or "I reckon I know."

Sims laughed and he shouted, "Well, prove it then." His words and his laughing voice, set thus about Imogene's story, were like a loud obscene rhyme sung abroad in the wheat. "Prove away," he said, "we're all here ready to know what 'tis. Say what you've got to say now once and for all and let's have it over. I'll say you another equal to any two tales you've got to tell. Tell it fast and I'll spread news of it over to Rudds's fields and farther when I go there after dinner to get the balance of the binden twine he promised to let us use. Whoop-law, Eliza, poor gal! Prove what's on your chest. I always said I'd like to hear one on Imogene. I never did."

Cundy muttered and raged, repeating all that he had said formerly of his daughter. Sims drove him to newer anger, but he seemed not to address him, as if these taunts were but the opinion which the tale Cundy had to tell of Imogene would arouse over the whole community. Cundy seemed scarcely able to speak, addressing Stoner.

"She's in a man's house, like she was his wife, and not married."

"I reckon she's married fair enough," Stoner said, trying to make peace. "The neighbors all thought it was a fair enough wedden."

"She's not married. She's not married to Wilson. I can prove it."

"I saw the license," Sims said.

"She's not married."

"I saw the license papers. I and Rudds were the signed witnesses. Go home and ease yourself," Sims speaking again.

"She's not married. Fifty licenses won't make a marriage iffen they're not served in a proper way. Old Turner has got no right to make a marriage ceremony. He's in default. He had such a right once but he lost it."

"Maybe Turner lost his rights, I don't know. I never heard of it," Stoner said, speaking gently, as if he would ask pardon for Imogene if she were in fault.

"In his house five days now, and not married. Let her go fast to the devil."

"You better come in and eat your dinner," Stoner said, breaking the spell of the unpleasant argument with this neighborly courtesy. "You better come on in to dinner." But Cundy left,

going back across the cut field toward the meadow
and then to the highroad, riding in a sharp walk,
as if he held some destination in mind.

A morning again, and the reaper was busy with
the wheat. The uncut grain was now but an uneven island in the middle of the field, and the
horses stepped quickly, urged because of the gathering clouds. At eleven o'clock the storm broke
and the shower fell. All the men and the beasts
hurried to shelter and the ground ran with a quick
flow of dashing water. Rain beat in at the windows
and wet the closed doors. The hens ran to the barn
for shelter, huddling there with drawn-in feathers,
making themselves small and close to expel the
damp. The dark cloud rolled northward, having
spilled this bright clatter of wet, having drenched
the grass at Blair's and Trigg's and Stoner's, and
when it had crossed the creek it turned back and
gathered anew, and a downpour fell on the farms
north of the creek, on Rudds's and Wilson's and
Cundy's.

The work of the farm having been stopped by
the shower, Ben walked out to the road, uncertain
whether he would go to Wilson's or to Blair's.
Withindoors the thieves were painting, the furni-

ture piled in the middle of the floors. Mr. and
Mrs. Stoner were sitting on the kitchen porch to
tell and retell their opinions of Cundy, of Turner,
of Philly Blair, and to wonder what Giles Wilson
had better do next. Ben stood in the road, thinking that he would like to go to Wilson's farm and
to Blair's, to both, to one or the other. At Wilson's
he would stand about in the barn lot and talk to
Giles about the shower and the possible damage it
might have brought to the wheat. Then he would
lower his voice and say, being fearful to mention
it, but willing, "What do you think about what
Cundy says? It's a queer thing, a father bound
he'll ruin his daughter's reputation. . . ." Wilson would stutter his reply, being confused and
angered, and he would say, "You'd better stay all
night. . . ." The hounds would be nosing about
in the fresh grass.

Ben climbed the fence opposite Stoner's house
and went uncertainly outward. He went over a
cornfield and into a pasture, but he stopped at the
ruined stump to prod the rotted wood with his
toe, and he laid his hands along the newly mended
fence to feel the staples, as if he would sniff the
wet earth for himself and find a new scent. He
walked then toward the small brown house that
was seen now, the roof crookedly lifted between

two hills. Inside it a kettle of gold rested under the hearthstone. The kettle and Imogene's plight, these were two drawing points that pulled at him evenly, and he walked uncertainly through the wet herbs, toward Blair's barn lot. He stood outside the garden fence and called "Hello," and Blair came to the door of the house to answer him.

Beyond the barn, far to the left, some tangled brush grew, and somewhere off in this wild part a guinea was making a "quatrack, quatrack," a cry that fell wild and sharp as a protest toward himself, a stranger to the farm. The Blairs were sitting inside, out of the wet.

"I made your guineas sing," Ben said. All the guineas were in a stir now, but their voices were gone farther, as if they had hidden in the thicket.

"They do everything else on the sly but sing," Mrs. Blair said. "You'd think their eggs would be made outen gold, the way they hide them off."

She was ready to talk, but the man, Andy Blair, went away, stalking off across the stepping stones toward the barn.

"It's trouble to find a guinea egg, that I know," Ben said. "And when you find it you have to take it out with care. Is that right?"

"You have to rob the guinea's nest with a spoon, and a right long-handled spoon too. They're a sight, the way they think their eggs are precious. I always said a guinea-hen is the touchiest kind that lays eggs at all."

"If you think anything is precious, it's a good thing to hide it deep. In this world that's so," Ben said. "I reckon the guinea-hens are a right smart kind. . . ."

"Is your name Shepherd? John B., maybe?" she asked.

"Shepherd, yes, but they call me Ben. Ben is what they call me by." He wanted to go back to talk of the guineas, but she was quick to run forward another matter.

"I know who you are," she said. "You came here to the party and to the wedden. How are you?"

"I'm at work at Stoner's," Ben said.

"He's had his house new painted, they say. Paint always makes a place look bright, I think. A painter, one of the men that painted there, came here Wednesday."

"Gracious Lord! What did he come here for?" Ben asked.

"He said he was through at Stoner's. Said he wanted another place to paint. He offered to paint this room here for four dollars and furnish all the paint besides. Wanted more work, he said. . . ."

"He's not half through at Stoner's." Ben spoke

in a whisper, as if some others might be listening. "He's got the whole outside to do again, the second coat. . . ."

"Then that man, the painter, I wouldn't trust his word. Nor his deed neither. What-for did he lie to me for?"

"He's apt to be a liar," Ben said. "Don't trust what he says."

"I won't let him come inside my door," she called out.

"His partner, the other one, Larkin, he's a boaster. He's a smooth talker. You might like to hear what he has to say. He'd talk to you half a day and you'd think he was a lonesome man away from home to find work."

"I wouldn't trust him neither," she said. "Iffen he makes a partnership with one that lies he's no better himself. I wouldn't trust a man like that. Don't let him come inside my door." She said that she must go to get the guinea eggs. She seemed half fearful of something. "Didn't you use to live out there?" she asked, pointing toward the north. "Is your name John B., maybe?" They talked about the ants and she went away out of the room suddenly and stayed away, but she came back to the doorway twice to peep within. Ben heard her walking about softly in the kitchen. When she did

not come back he went to the kitchen and then to
the place beside the well, just outside the kitchen
door. She said that she must go to the guineas and
she caught up a pail and a spoon and stepped
quickly away toward the thicket. Looking back
from the pasture Ben saw her watching his departure as she peered out from among the bushes.

As he expected, Ben had a summons to come
home at the end of the week, the message coming
from his father and telling him that he had tarried
from home long enough, that he was needed there.
It was a mandatory message, allowing no delay and
fixing the morning of the next day as the last time
he might spend from home. The long twilight
had begun; the bats were beginning to dart about
the trees above Stoner's house, and the swallows
had flown headlong into the chimney. The work
for the week was done, and the cutting tools were
housed in the barn for the coming of the Sabbath,
the work-horses turned out to the pasture where
they would rest themselves with a Sabbath plenty
of grass. Ben went away from the farm, bidding
the farmer and his wife good-bye, and when he
had walked for a little along the highroad, going
outward and away from the village, as if he were

a traveler, he left the road and turned back across a hill. He had a wish to visit the stream once more and the place where he had camped. The night-jars were busy in the sky and the long twilight continued. The cocks at the farmsteads here and there were crowing now and then at the long strange dusk. The longest day of the year was passing to its late evening.

He crossed the creek at the watergap and went up the stream toward the camping-place. He had not sent the bone to Robbie May, and now it seemed as if a determination not to send it had washed over his mind. He took the bone from the little box and threw the box away into the herbs, putting the bone back into his pocket. He cared nothing for her now, as if in the hour of his de-parture he had shed her and all her works from his mind, and likewise he had shed Bonnie, who had been good to him. He left them to their own living devices, wishing them no harm. He won-dered, all his thought in a shadow, how he had ever devised the plan to send the bone, since the message it conveyed was unfaith with Bonnie for whom he had crossed his heart and body and hoped he would die if ever he revealed what she told him. His hate being dispersed, it was strange to him that he had not remembered his oath.

His pride had made him forget. Now pride
was diffused, being viewed as an abstract,
no more of importance than hunger or cruelty
or mirth.

"I am the seventh generation from Tobias," he
said.

While he stood thus at the side of a thorn bush,
on the bluff above the place where he had camped,
he saw two men come from the highroad and pass
toward Blair's pasture. They shuffled in and out
among the bushes, one walking behind the other,
and they stopped at the blackberry bushes to eat
the ripened fruit. Ben watched them, half in a
dream, and he began to unsay each part of the
note he had written to accompany the bone, to
undo the spell and malice of it. "You have got a
proud back and a pretty face" was allowed to
stand one instant until he had obliterated the evil
that was meant to hinge upon it. . . . "My cousin
ten steps removed" was carefully unwound and
undone, and the kinship canceled. "You do not
want to dance with a wraith now, but some day
you may need to" came next, to be carefully with-
drawn and untied, strand and knot, charm and
letter. Only the last sentence was left now, and
this, apart from the rest, had no sinister meanings,
"I recommend on that day this bone." He would

take the bone back to its place. He would not try
to destroy it, since he could not. It would go back
where it had lain.

The men who had been eating the berries came
farther into the pasture, and from their shapes
and outlines he knew that they were Larkin and
Grove. He followed them a little way up the rise
and he saw that they kept among the bushes at the
edge of the enclosure. They went past the old
work-horse that grazed not far from the fence.
When they came to the end of the tall growth
Grove remained hidden among the tangle of
boughs, but Larkin went forward alone. Ben
wanted to follow, but the summons hung heavily
over his will and he must do the bidding of his
father.

He must go back to the grave before the light
of the day was entirely gone. He wanted more than
the moonlight to light him into the leafy cavern
where the bones were scattered. Uncertain, wanting to follow the rogues to see what they were devising, he still kept to his own necessity, and he
turned back, stepping lightly, recrossing the hill.
Three bats darted about in the air, circling his
head. Their passage was as light as the faint wind
of twilight and their turnings and glidings were
swift, made by the gossamer lightness of their pli-

able wings. Thus attended he went back toward the stream.

A deep redness lingered after the setting of the sun, spreading up from the ground in the western point and hanging a strange curtain there. The moon was already bright in the east, being full. Ben crossed the creek on the stones not far from the watergap, the water being low, and he went up the bluff on the opposite side, toiling among the briars, not looking to find a path or a crooked stair of ledges and stones. On the top he walked northward over the pastures and skirted the edge of a field until he came to the old Shepherd burying-place.

There the moonlight came brightly over the stones, and no lettering being required of them, they seemed clear and sharp, as if they told clear legends. He had been into the homes of the living Shepherds, they now wearing other names, and he had seen them at their working, their living, their play, their lovings. He had walked through their old orchards and among their bees, and he had stripped their seedling grass and cut their wheat. He had fished in their stream and trapped their game in the thickets. He had surprised them at forbidden love; he had eaten their food; and he had prayed with them in their church. Here there was a gay humor over the stones, for the light of the moon and the waning day met with the whiteness of the rocks.

There was no human outcry, none crying "Mine," or "Nine." He dreamed over this remote memory, without malice, letting it become undone and unstated. His passage through the brush was not difficult. In the small inner glade the daylight and the moonlight were dim, but he found his way, and he laid the bone down in the place where it used to lie.

V

ON THE MORNING AFTER THE WEDDING, PHILLY, lying in the bed above-stairs, waked and slept, arising and falling, knowing and not knowing. As she waked a heaviness pressed upon her, fatigue and the heaviness of many cares, until the roof and the walls seemed to lie upon her breast. Under this weight she in turn bore down upon the bed and the floor, upon the hearth, holding down the stone, and in the midst lay the breath of her throat as a light leaf floating. The leaf came into being, or it went out altogether. Her distressed flesh ached in long lines of pain that became long thin bones of weariness and hurt, slim little splinters of hard pain-substance that lay under her flesh. Her knotty finger-bones were crumpled, shut with her hands, as if they would hold tight to their share. Her foot-bones were stretched out stiff, spreading toward the end of the bed, wanting bindings to hold them together, wanting some narrow bed to lie in.

Waking thus long after sunrise, she scarcely noticed Andy as he went about his morning work. She persuaded herself in the moment of her last waking that nothing unusual or unallowed had come to the house, that it was no matter what vessel might lay hidden under some hearth. Every house held its secret and private matters. The strangeness of the kettle had become the everyday measure of her life. She concerned herself rather with the predicament into which she had persuaded Imogene and the hurried wedding, and she began to fear Mr. Cundy. He would, she told herself, as she drew on her clothing, be in a great rage over the loss of his daughter during the season of the harvest when there would be extra men to be fed, beside himself and the four hungry boys. Cundy farmed in a very extensive way, she remembered anew, for he had many fields. The harvesters would be at work there for a week, she told herself again, as she stirred her fire and saw the kettle begin to throw up a thin ribbon of steam. It being Sunday morning, there would be a great clutter in Cundy's deserted kitchen, the men going awkwardly in and out, and old Cundy himself would be trying to fry the bacon and stir the corn batter for breakfast.

She expected Cundy to come to her door in anger and she prepared speeches to offer him. He would push the door open and walk in, spreading the door wide as he came and keeping his hand on the latch, as if he were there only to thrust his anger within. He could get himself a cook in a right way, she argued. His large red face would be purple where the blood of his rage had clotted under the skin. He would lift his great right hand, his left hand still on the latch of the spread door. Eyes like Imogene's would look out of his head, but his mouth would be larger and more full. The floor would creak under his weight. He need not think he could hold Imogene all her life, she told him, her head twisting suddenly over her task. She threshed the matter about in mind, her head tossing and her chin snapping up and down over her short words, making imaginary replies to his angry argument. He could marry himself a cook. There were women a-plenty. She named three to satisfy her argument. There were warm creeping sensations moving about through the top of her spine and mounting to renewed anger whenever she thought of Imogene as married forcefully, as being obliged to steal away for her happiness.

Going with Imogene into her married morning, she saw her in Giles Wilson's house. Outside were the long rows of beehives. She would call her former home by the telephone line and she would talk with one of her brothers or with her father, if his rage would let him speak civilly. A clank of iron on the stones behind the well-house, toward the barn—Giles himself going down to milk the cows. Imogene would be picking up the scattered parts of Giles's life and bringing them together. The old hounds would be shy of her and they would stay far from the house, or if they came for their bread they would hold their heads low, as if they were ashamed. While he walked down the stone path to the barn, Giles would be remembering continually that she was in the house and the memory would be as a flower in his bosom.

Thus Philly contrived for Imogene. Sunday passed in a routine of rest and labor. Toward dusk she began to think of the little pouch which held the two round pearls and to wonder that Andy had kept them in secret, that he had not spoken of them to her. When she was in the bed she thought of them, wondering to hear Andy breathe aloud beside her that he would hold the pearls as somehow more secret than the kettle and that he had

not told her what he would do with them. She
pretended to sleep, but all the while she waited,
listening to Andy's breath, and when he lay
heavily, scarcely breathing in the depths of rest,
toward midnight, she touched his body lightly
with quick cunning fingers and explored it for
some signs of the pearls. Across his back ran a tape
or string, and when she followed this about his
body until it rested on the fore part of his trunk
she found that it came to an end with a little knot,
and from the knot there extended downward another thread from which hung a small sack of
cloth, the little pouch in which the pearls were
tied. She let her fingers play lightly with the two
small round beads inside the cloth, cautious, her
touch deft as the blowing of an aspen leaf, for
the pouch rested on Andy's skin, hanging below
the belt. It gave her a delight to touch the pearls
thus, as if she had put her hand into the kettle
itself and had fingered the riches there. Three
times during the night she let her hand find the
little treasure and finger it lightly, and each time
she could count the two pearls, saying, "This one
and that one," knowing that they were real and
that the kettle was real. They were a near and
present symbol of the wealth in the kettle and she
touched them with delight. But she did not know

clearly why Andy carried them thus or why he had hidden them from her unless he wished thus to increase his value in his own eyes by adding these bits of precious treasure to his own person to make up somehow for whatever he lacked. Or perhaps, she thought, as she drowsed happily to her own rest, he merely wished to have a symbol of the kettle always within reach, to be fingered at any moment.

On Monday, seeing far into Wilson's house where Imogene moved softly about, Philly had a renewed interest in her own kitchen and hen-yard. Across two or more miles of rolling hills Imogene would be making the bed, airing the linen, or she would be making curds to feed the little chicks. Philly set upon her own labors, matching Imogene, and she sang a loud song as she worked. It was a secret delight to her that she had found Andy's private hiding-place and that she knew where he had hidden the little pouch. He had gone to the field early and he worked there as if he would tear the earth asunder. With the sack tied to his middle and hidden deeply away where it touched his flesh continually, he was increased. From the window of the kitchen she saw him rolling the mower over his hay field, sending the horse steadily across the patch of hay. She baked the common little cake that he liked best to eat. It was not the tall elegant man who had tied the little sack across his middle, but the old one, knotty and hard-jointed. She had a merry song in her throat while she scoured her milk tin and baked the sweetened sponge that Andy liked.

She dipped her brush-stick into her snuff can and set the fine powder, all tasseled on the end of the brush, against her teeth, matching her merry mood again with this frivolity. She sat beside the door for a little to allow the faint pleasure engendered to flow over her throat and her breast. "Let Robbie May and Bonnie and Effie Trigg, and Imogene even, let all get whatever they can outen their sweethearts under the lilac bushes or wherever . . ." She spat lightly into the grass. "Which one amongst them all has got a man that's got two fine pearls in a little sack that hangs from his waist, close to his skin? Which one wouldn't trade what they'll get for what old Andy has got to hide against his middle part?" She spat a fine thin spray in a swift arc and sat shaking lightly with her musings and her inner laughter.

The little dip-stick in the corner of her lips, she went out among the hens, carrying them food and water. Her pleasure in the care of the hens turned about to meet her in the fragrant air that floated downward from the great tulip tree that grew over the hen-yard. She was rid now of her anxiety for the pot and her fear of Cundy. She went to the tool-house and found a hammer and some nails and she determined that she would mend the hen-house roof herself.

She climbed to the top of the hen-house, going first to the top of a little pig-house from which she could reach the higher roof. She drew herself up with many efforts, worming and crawling until she had a firm hold upon the upper boards. Working upward and clinging, she came at last to a firm seat on the top of the roof.

There was much to do there. The boards were old and rotted, many of them out of place. When she had rested she began to drive the nails and to settle the boards about. Fresh breezes continued to blow from the tulip tree and some careless little bird sang again and again among the wide-reaching boughs, twittering when the hammer stopped its din. Philly had a great joy now in what she did, the little dip-stick beating lightly with her mutterings.

"I said to Andy twenty times, said, 'How about the roof to the hen-house. . . .' " Muttering anew, after driving two nails, " 'Iffen they lived out in nature and had to scratch for every bite they eat, they wouldn't be so particular,' Andy says. 'They better be thankful for what they've got. A good safe place to live in,' he says. Men are a half-wit set. Plumb crazy in the head, I sometimes think." She drew the boards into place and drove nails into them, puzzled over the set of one or the lack of another, nailing, searching, fitting part to part. Andy liked to tell all the old things he had told, over and over. She could usually tell what he intended to say when first he began a speech. But while she drove the nails she saw a new thing about Andy. She could foretell what he would say when he began a speech, but when he said nothing there was a curious thing, as if it would be a mystery about him or near him. "And Andy's old over-and-over talk is as good as what is said new, and is all the same as the new, when you sift down to rock bottom," she muttered at last.

The wood was soft and the nails went into it easily, so that driving the hammer up and down was not difficult. Muttering again, she puzzled over the fit of a plank: "He don't drink nohow and he don't owe a debt in the world. . . . Andy never yet, after all, drove me to tears, and you can't say that about all the balance. . . . I recollect Lispy Cundy cried all of a summer, before her tears dried up in her and she couldn't cry any more. . . . I never had any real call to cry. . . . But I take care not to."

The hens kept far away from their house, suspicious of the noise that came from the roof. The guineas cried out their frightened "quatrack" and then were still, having hidden far in the thicket.

She had driven all the nails but four or five and she began to feel a distrust of the roof, for there were still spaces that were uncovered. She sat very still, resting her arm, and she looked about on the quiet hen-yard. Resting, she had a new fullness of pleasure well up within her to be sitting thus, away from the walls of the house, away from Andy and the knowledge which they held together of what lay under the hearth. She saw the old hound running off toward the upper field. It was pleasant to be there, to breathe the fresh cool air that swept through the tulip tree, to rest her arm, her hand free of the hammer, careless, carefree, thinking nothing, rid of danger, shed of malice and pride, drowsed by the spent dip-brush and the warm air of the midday.

Then she saw the hen which she called the "old pullet," stepping cautiously across the hen-yard,

going toward the hen-house, stepping forward and
stopping to listen. Philly kept very still, knowing
that the old pullet wanted to lay an egg. There
was something strange about this fowl, something
which Philly had never been able to discover.
She had a suspicion of her, and she thought that
now she might watch this one and find her out.

"I always suspicioned that pullet," Philly whispered. "I always wanted to find out what her
tricks are." She met the sly caution of the fowl
with her own sly caution, sitting in quiet while
the hen stepped nearer.

The hen went slowly through the door and
Philly lay on the roof and fixed her eyes at one of
the cracks so that she could watch all that went
forward inside. The hen went slowly over the floor
of the room, watching, listening, driven forward
by the heaviness of life that pushed her where
she would as leave not go. She went cautiously over
the dusty floor of the room below and jumped
carefully to the frame that held the nest. She
looked about once more, peering here and there,
and settled then to the straw and closed her eyes
to wait.

While Philly watched the hen, her face pressed
close to the boards of the roof and her eyes
strained to see through the cleft, a vivid image,

sharp in outline and highly colored, came boldly before her concern about the hen and floated in and out of her inner vision, as if she were straining to see it. It was a kettle of money and precious stones, bright gold and silver coins put into an iron pot and two fine pearls tied into a little sack. She blinked twice and pushed her nose into the opening to dispel the image, to have a little rest from it. In the next instant she knew the evil that surrounded the old pullet. When the fowl had laid the egg she stood over it and began to peck at it with her bill. When she had made a hole in the shell she supped out the inner part.

Soon afterward the hen came from the nest in a wide arc, flying and fluttering, throwing out a great broken bleat of joy and fright that brought all the other hens to a cackling chorus. Philly had a momentary sickness spread over her, and she remembered Cundy in spite of her concern for the roof. She saw Cundy pressing his large mouth into the egg to sup out the sweet inner part. She had a distaste for all that she had done during the morning and she began to descend, scarcely looking once at the makeshift roof she had tried to devise. When she had lowered her body over the ledge and had rested a little while on the top of the pig-house, she walked across the

hen-yard, and halfway across she met the old
pullet walking drowsily about, looking for water
with which to dilute the rich and evil feast she
had enjoyed.

Noon had come. Philly went to the house, and
turning about quickly among her tasks, she went
once to the parlor to see if the clock had stopped.
The day seemed unjointed and delayed. The old
pullet had eaten a hole into the morning; she had
bitten with her hard bill a flaw into the steady
world that lay outside the new world of the kettle.
She had made a crack in time itself and in the
illusions people hold together. Throughout the
afternoon Philly was weary from the work of the
morning and the act of the old pullet. She was
hushed and spent in mind, saddened and alarmed.
She sat outside the house during the afternoon and
rested under the honey-locust tree, in a place
where she had seldom sat before.

Waking in the night, while Andy slept, she explored his flesh with light fingers that scarcely
touched anything, and she found again the tape
about his waist. At the end of it still hung the
little lump and the two pearls were still inside.
When she had touched them enough and had felt
that they were actually two she drew her hand
cautiously away and fell asleep.

On Wednesday, in the afternoon, she took up her own again, letting the old pullet and all that she provoked go into a void. Then she despised the half-patched hen-house roof and remembered the rotting boards into which she had foolishly driven nails during the whole of a morning. When she had cleared her kitchen, Andy being at hand, she began to speak freely of the needs of the hens. She openly discussed the party and the wedding, naming those who had come and repeating opinions that had been spoken. She brought the party and the pot of gold vividly back to mind and set them boldly before Andy. He sat in his chair, uneasily shifting before the power of her picturing speech.

"I didn't hear you name your good luck today," she began. "You almost lost your pot of gold, Andy Blair." She walked about the room, naming the guests. "Callie sits in this chair here and Hez Turner stands alongside the wall, and Robbie May dances over here in a corner. I recollect all as well as you do yourself. Hester Trigg sits out near the middle of the floor, as hearty as life itself, with her pink cheeks, and her hands are in her lap."

"A fine looker enough, she is," Andy said. "A hearty woman with a still tongue a part of the time."

"I thought you didn't favor to invite Hester," Philly called back.

"I didn't care iffen she came. All is, I said once married ought to be enough to content a woman."

"I see all the men jump when she says she wants the lamp wick turned lower. You too, Andy."

"All I cared, Philly, was to turn down the smoke outen the chimney."

"I never said she wasn't a fine looker. I told you so last week and always. Pink in her cheeks and her breath short and quick where she's quick in her heart. When she dies it'll be sudden, in a stroke, but not soon likely."

"It'll be all the same to me," Andy said. "I don't care whe'r nor which about it. She's got right good sense, though."

"I'm in a fidget old man Cundy might come here over Imogene and Giles." Philly turned to the more important matter, the opening of the kettle. "He might get the law on his side and come here yet with the sheriff."

"Imogene is of a consenten age," Andy said. "He can't use the law to make trouble."

"He's sure to come though, as mad as a hornet. 'What call have you got, Philly Blair, to marry Imogene outen my house right now, harvest time and eight men to cook for, right when I need Imogene most?' Hear him say it."

"Well," Andy said, speaking in a weak way, "what call did you have? I didn't say for Giles and Imogene to get married now in harvest time. Iffen he comes it's you he'll have a grudge against, and you can find your own way out."

"Lord-a-mighty! hear Andy Blair talk. Iffen Imogene wasn't married to Giles now at this minute where'd you and your kettle of money be? 'Lay your whole pocketbook on the altar,' he says, and you beside yourself for fear you'd give all you had then and there. Ten minutes more, Andy Blair, and you would 'a' repented in Hez Turner's way and joined Hez Turner's religion, and that's a religion where you give up all you've got. I see you beat the air with your fists and say, 'I know I'm a sinful man,' and Turner stands over you and tells you what to do to get shed of what is a-binden you. It's a religion that's swallowed down a many's the small little pocketbook before now, and it's not apt to stand back before a kettle of gold, neither."

Andy was quiet, looking at his hands that lay twisted together. Philly let the argument lie quietly for a time, seeing that he was disturbed, that he lay under the spell of her thrusting voice. Presently he said, speaking in a distraught way:

"Cundy is already in a ragen fit, bound he'll make mischief. I hear he gives Imogene a bad name and makes a mystery over her. He tells on her the worst you could tell on a woman. That's what I hear today."

Philly thought of this, turning it about in quiet. She spoke sadly, thinking to finish the argument. "I promised Imogene a wedden with fancy things to eat. It turned out so's I couldn't have it and now she's married to save your pot under the hearth-rock. I'm in a mind to give Imogene a present. Some dinnerware would be nice, I always think. I'm a mind to buy a little present of some china-ware for Imogene and Giles, a white ground with little blue flowers."

"I don't know what call I'm got to buy crockery for Giles Wilson's kitchen," Andy said. He stood up in the floor now, as if he had found a point at which to make resistance, as if he were having the last word. He made as if he would take up his hat from the floor and go out. "Nobody as I ever knew ever bought any tinware and such truck for my house, and I'll not see my way to buy for Giles Wilson. Let Wilson furnish out his own house plunder."

"You are of a short memory, Andy," she said. "Ten minutes ago you had in mind how you almost gave up the whole pot and how Imogene, unknown to herself, saved you. And now you've forgot. And whatever you do or don't do, the henhouse is bound to have a new roof. I couldn't mend another mend to the old one, so rotten it is it can't turn water. I aim to have a little part of what's inside the pot and iffen you can't help me get what's wanted I might pry up the stone and have out what I need without help. I'm a strong woman when my head's set. It makes a new strength come to my arms. A new roof to the henhouse is what I want."

"You are a fast-talken woman, that I know," he said, leaving. "A man is put-to to try to keep up with what you say."

"Suppose Hez Turner would come back here again," she held him with her uplifted finger, "suppose he comes to see you out in the hay and nobody at hand to help you out. Suppose I invite him to come. 'Come over to see Andy again, he's troubled in his mind,' I'll say. . . . Recollect last Saturday night? Callie sits here and Imogene over yonder and Hester sits in the middle. Then Hez Turner comes up and says his customary say, 'Lay your pocketbook on the altar, Andy Blair,' and

everybody stands back, amazed to see what a state
he's got you into. Lay your whole pocketbook on
the altar, Andy Blair. It's your pocketbook is your
stumblen block. Open up your hearth-rock and
dig out what you've got under there. Lay your
money pot on the altar." She was standing over
him to admonish. "Give up all. Give over everything. Lay your kettle of old money out on the
floor for all the people to grab some. You are a
very easy man for Hez Turner's kind, Andy Blair.
You heard a voice speak once, didn't you? Hez
Turner will lay hands on you yet and make you
give up everything you've got. I won't have a girl
handy to marry off to save your skin, neither. Girls
in a mood to marry are not handy come by, the
same time there's men with licenses in hand, all
ready. It's not customary."

"I never said I wouldn't take outen the pot
money to mend the hen-house roof, Philly. You
never heard me say I wouldn't. It'll take all new
boards. I'll get Lige Dover to saw me out some
boards right away. I always like poplar iffen I
can get it. Poplar is the best log for lumber, and
that's what my better judgment always told me to
use." He talked about the poplar boards he had
used in building the barn and told where they
were cut, easing himself from the pressing need

of the hen-house behind this ancient story. He went a long way with the story of the barn, and back of that into an account of a sawmill that used to stand near Beech Fork, lost in one of his old over-and-over stories.

While Andy was thus recounting there came a knock at the door, the front door of the house, which had been closed since the guests had passed through it. Now a low, tentative knock fell on the door, falling twice when Andy delayed to open. Philly looked up in alarm, knowing that no neighbor would announce himself thus. A neighbor would call "Hello" from the gate and proclaim his goodwill before he touched the door panels. While Andy and Philly looked, one toward the other, and shifted about in their places in fright, the knock sounded again, a steady, respectful beat, so soft that the guineas had not heard. Then Andy walked to the door and opened it.

Grove, the house-painter, stood beyond the doorstep. He carried two pails and some brushes and he stepped from one foot to the other, as if he would seem to have just walked up to the door, as if he were still walking.

"I heard you wanted your house painted," he said. "I came to see what it was you wanted painted." Here he bit his jaws together and swallowed, beginning his speech anew. "I'll make a neat job," he said. "Paint I had left from my last job . . ." He made a long speech, wanting to be allowed to paint the house.

"I don't want any paint," Andy called out. "I never told anybody I wanted a painter."

"I'll do this room here, all for five dollars," Grove said to them, insisting. "All the woodwork inside, and furnish the paint."

"It's good enough for me," Andy said, declining the offer. "I never told a soul I wanted paint. I'm in no mind to paint now. You make a waste of your words when you ask me."

Grove came up the last step to the doorsill and looked into the room. "I was here Saturday night and I said to my partner, 'This room needs paint.' I'll do all for four dollars and furnish all the paint to do it with."

"I've got no mind to paint," Andy said again and again. Grove came further into the room and looked about as if he measured the length and breadth of it. He argued for the painting, offering again to do the work for four dollars.

"We don't want any painten done," Philly said

to him. She hurried about the room now, pulling the chairs this way and that as if she were setting them to rights. "Mr. Blair, you can take the man outside the door and talk all you want. I'm of a mind to lay me down now to rest myself. I'll just lay me down on this sofa and make the room dark for a spell."

The men went outside and Philly locked the door, and she peeped out from behind the closed blinds. The stranger walked entirely around the house, looking upward toward the roof, looking at the foundation, pointing and talking. Andy kept beside the man as he walked about and he scarcely hid his ill humor. Peeping from the darkened window crevice, Philly saw the intruder go at last.

Andy went about through the dusk listening. "What's to hear now, Philly?" he would ask, leaning forward. The kettle was not mentioned in their speech, nor did Philly recall the party again. Outside the twilight lingered and the mockingbird sang even after moonrise. The house seemed lonely and undefended, set apart in the summer dusk. After supper was eaten, Andy, whispering, told what he had planned. They would drag a heavy chest of drawers from the opposite wall and stand it partly over the hearth so that it would cover the stone under which the kettle was hidden. When this labor was finished they locked the doors and windows, closing the shutters tight, and they went, hushed, above-stairs to sleep.

In the night Philly fingered again for the sack of pearls, wanting comfort. Her hand went lightly to Andy's side and moved up and down over his hip to find the little tape that would lead to the small treasure. She thought that she must have fallen asleep in the search, for her hand had found nothing. Then she stirred lightly to assure herself that she was awake, and she set upon the task more carefully. But her fingers met nothing which might be a thread or a tape or a string. She began to tremble, so that her touch was less light, and she rested for a little from the search until she had assured herself that the pearls were surely in the place they had formerly been. When she was still and light again she went swiftly over the whole of Andy's middle, over his trunk and his legs, but there was no tape and no little sack of pearls. She felt then at his neck and his breast, his arms and his ankles, but there was nothing.

She slept then, fearfully and without comfort, unsatisfied and saddened. She had laid no claim to the pearls beyond the secret comfort they gave when she fingered them in the night and the pleasant thought of Andy as having them thus on his person to enhance him wherever he lacked. By the middle of the morning, having satisfied herself that the little sack was not in the house, she began to think that Andy had given it to somebody, and on the instant that this thought appeared it seemed clear to her that he had given it to Hester Trigg, for Hester could easily get the best that any man had.

When she tried to piece together Andy's life since the beginning of the week and to account for each hour of it she found that, being busy with her own matters, she had not known, hour by hour, whether he worked in his fields or went toward the village. He would meet Hester on the road and give her, at first, only a blunt courtesy. But Hester had a comfortable way and she could endure any amount of rudeness, having been married twice. It would be naught to her that Andy gave her a hard and short "Good-morning," walking past her. She would say some sensible thing, of the sort a man likes, and he would turn back to answer her. By the time they came to her house she would be telling of the fine cherries she had gathered, the tree being of some rare and peculiar sort, little known in the country. Then she would offer to give him a cherry pie from the new cherry

tree and her own rare baking, and he would go
inside her house.

She had no anger for the loss of the pearls from
Andy's side, but rather a sadness that he might
have given them to Hester. If he gave them to
some young girl or even to some pretty wanton
in the town she would not have cared, but rather
would have been proud of him as being able to
do what a man naturally does. The tall fine man
in elegant clothing had nothing to do with this
transaction, for she had felt the pearls actually
upon Andy's flesh against his angular hip and his
flat stomach. Thinking about over the whole
country, she named each woman above the age of
childhood, and she tested her feelings, finding
that she did not mind if Andy gave the pearls to
any one of them, except Hester. Hester would be
secret about the gift itself, but she would take
more comfort to herself and have a pride in being
able to get from any man all that he had.

On Thursday in the afternoon Philly heard the
voices of women outside her door, and presently
Ronnie Rudds was calling without. Philly's breath
leaped with fear and pleasure when she thought
that now she would surely have news of Imogene.

The women came inside the door and chose the chairs they liked to sit in, Emma Trigg sinking into the rocking-chair and Eliza White taking the small chair near the door.

"The heat's a sight," Emma said. She was very large and heavy and warm. "A body can't hardly get a good breath for it."

"But summer's here, and what else can you expect?" The heat did not trouble her because she was quick and thin. She knew that the women had something of a mighty importance to tell.

"I see you've moved some furniture," Eliza said, looking at the chest that stood beside the fireplace.

"It's always nice to have a difference between summer and winter in the way you set the furniture, I always think," Philly replied to them.

"It makes you know when summer comes," Ronnie began to say, "makes you know a difference between summer and winter."

"Which one is it wants to get married?" Philly asked, making a joke. They were all the mothers of large families, married long ago.

They laughed and Eliza said, "Nobody really wants to." Emma Trigg laughed so hard at this that her reply was lost, but Ronnie Rudds spoke louder than the rest and later, saying, "Everybody wants to get married, don't they?"

"Has anybody seen Imogene since Saturday?" Philly asked suddenly. "What did her old daddy say when she married Giles?" She looked hard at Eliza, knowing that there would be some fearful thing to tell.

"It's past belief either Giles or Imogene ever fixed up such a surprise," Emma cried out. "Some ways it seems Andy must 'a' fixed it up. It's past belief."

"Whyn't you go see Imogene and ask her how 'twas? Ask her how come it was Giles ever got any license, firstplace."

"You can't go against nature, I always found," Emma Trigg said.

"You can't go against, no. You have to go along with. You have to in a manner ease yourself along with nature." Ronnie Rudds offered this explanation.

"Or else," Eliza said, "you have to ignore nature. Not take any notice to nature. Just let yourself ease along. Let nature go his way and you go your way. Live and let live."

"What we want to know is how it ever came in your mind to do such a thing, and how you ever got the courage to go straight against Sam Cundy. It was dangerous to do so, Philly."

"She's my own cousin's girl-baby, and her own

mammy dead. I'm the one, seems like, to help in her marryen, her father's house not got a woman in it. It seems fitten for her to marry in my house," Philly said, speaking shortly.

"It was a good day's work Philly and Andy did when they got Imogene outside Sam Cundy's house," Ronnie said. "We all say that. But the work is not done yet. There's more to do, Philly. There's another day's work yet, and not such an easy job, neither."

"Well," Philly said, "name what 'tis. I'll do my share and more. What's yet to do?"

She got up from her chair and began to walk around the room. She felt as if she were about to move the furniture again. If these women would show her what wanted moving she would set to work upon it. She wanted something to do, something that would require her strength and her speed. She walked up and down, placing things to rights, and she demanded what was amiss.

Ronnie began to tell her. Cundy said Imogene was not married to Giles. She counted on her fingers, bending down each finger slowly. Five days Imogene had been in Giles's house now, and not married to him in a right way, Cundy said. He had told what was lacking that very morning in Stoner's wheat field where Ed Sims and others

were cutting the grain. Giles had license papers
in a right way, and all that part was legal enough,
but Turner had not the right to serve the license.
Cundy was bound he'd have Giles in jail for a
crime. There would be a name to fit the deed,
but Ronnie did not know how to call it. "Breach
of the Peace" hardly seemed enough to name it
with. "Disorderly Conduct" might name the
offense, she thought.

"Then why wouldn't Giles get married again,
to suit the law?" Philly asked. "Why wouldn't he?"

"He says he's married enough and he'll not aim
to keep on marryen just to please Sam Cundy.
That's what he sent back for a reply to Cundy."

"Said iffen Sam Cundy wanted any more marryen he could try to find a lady and do it for his
own self."

"And Imogene, she said she'd do whatever Giles
did. Said he was her husband now, and iffen he
wanted to get married over again it was all the
same to her. Or if not, all the same. Whatever he
decided was what she would do."

"Why wouldn't Turner have the right?" Philly
asked, looking at the difficulty in another way.

"He could have the right iffen he'd go before
the County Court Clerk and made a bond . . ."

"Between three stubborn men, I reckon Imogene is in sin, and there she is," Philly called out.

She felt a great rush of words hammering at her throat, pushing themselves outward faster than she could say them with sense. She walked quickly about the room and she said that Cundy was a brute, no better than a beast in his own barn, and she remembered the old pullet and her nausea when she witnessed this fowl at her evil work. She said that there would always be a few who would get the tale wrong and would remember it vaguely and twist it about to do Imogene hurt. Then she went outside and pumped a bucket of cold water from the well and had a deep draught. She brought a pitcher of the cold water to her guests and found a teacup for them to drink from. "What then will we do?" she asked. "I'll go to see Imogene and Giles my own self."

She said that she would go at once. She would go to see Cundy himself, to see Turner. She would talk to Giles. It was a distress to her that there should be any flaw in Imogene's marriage or any whisper of shame about her, right or wrong. While she talked the women began to advise waiting. It would be best, they said, not to give too much importance to the matter. Let the angers cool away and let there be another wedding, if it were needed to satisfy the whole of the law, but the law would look out for itself and everything on that side would shape itself right.

"The law always looks out for itself, I always take notice," Eliza said.

"And the men stir themselves and look out for the law, iffen you ever noticed."

"Men are keen after law. The law won't suffer. We don't need to bother ourselves about the law part to it."

"Turner, he's run off, gone clear outen the country," Ronnie said.

"That makes it worse'n ever," Philly burst out.

"He'll come back," Eliza said, and Emma then:

"He's been gone before to parts unknown, but he always comes back."

"I don't care iffen he stays forever," Philly spoke after they had sat in silence for a short space of time. "But what became of the license paper Giles had here?" She remembered suddenly that she herself had held the license in her hands.

"There was a part on the end of the paper that Turner would have to fill in with his own hand, and then he'd have to take it to the County Court Clerk. It's that part on the paper that gave the trouble." Ronnie began to explain what was wanting, and Emma burst into the explanation, rocking hard now.

"It says, 'I qualified and gave bond, according to the law . . .' and Hez Turner never in his life qualified all the way for anything."

"Lester Rudds went to Turner's house after Turner left, and he found the paper, and there it was for a fact, filled in down to the place where the person that performed the ceremony had to begin, and after that it was only blank lines. And there's a little piece down at the bottom that says if the paper is not brought back to the Clerk in ninety days the man that makes the ceremony is to be fined fifty dollars."

"But iffen Turner never performed any ceremony, how can you tell where the ninety days is to start or end?" Eliza asked.

"That makes it still worse," Philly cried out. "I don't care whe'r Turner comes back or not, he's not qualified."

"Iffen Turner never made a marriage the ninety days has got not one thing to do with it, and there's worse'n fifty dollars to worry about for him."

"It's all crooked and twisted," Emma said. She began to rock lightly, as if she were done with it. "First Philly is sorry Turner's gone and she says that makes it worse'n ever, and then she's glad he's out of the way and don't care whe'r he comes or stays. It's all crooked and twisted and you can't tell right from wrong or up from down."

"It's twisted and bent till I can't see right ways from wrong ways, neither," Eliza speaking.

"One way you look at it and it seems Giles and Imogene are not married and all the neighborhood is in a stir," Ronnie said, in summary. "Other ways it's ne'er a thing to worry anybody and nobody cares nohow. There's up where down ought to be and inside is the same as outside. There's a plenty to do, but no very clear way to go about it. 'Breach of the Peace' and 'Disorderly Conduct' are floaten around in Sam Cundy's head, and as apt as not the sheriff, Bob Dragoo, might come out to see Giles, or Cundy might shoot Giles or Philly Blair, one or the other. And I've got to go home now and feed my little chickens. I had two hens come off yesterday with thirty-five."

They left, and Philly was quiet all during the evening. She did not wish to discuss Imogene's married state or Cundy's anger until she had thought out an attitude for herself or a plan to follow. She sat outside the door for a little while after supper, in the long twilight, and she talked with Andy of the rust blight that sometimes comes to the wheat, being thankful with him that there was little or none this season.

Philly was hushed and secret, deciding that she would wait, that she would say little of the mishap. As the report lay quietly resting now in her mind, she approached it as it were on tiptoe. Her thought was full of a whispered "let be" or "so and so" or "anyway and however." The whereabouts of the two pearls was still unknown to her. She let this mystery stand before the mishap of the wedding and she contrived to hush one secret with the wonder of the other. Her thought plucked lightly now and then at the thing wanting solution. It might come about that Turner had the right to perform marriage ceremonies, and then all the stir would be for nothing. It would be better then that nothing had been said. Let the people say to themselves, "What fools people are. What a stir over nothing." She would go nowhere. She would make no matter of it. She would say "hush" to her fidgety thought. Thus she tossed the matter lightly from her.

Underneath these conclusions another more serious annoyance appeared. It would seem, if the event had miscarried, that she should have made the wedding with more care, that she should have found a suitable minister, one empowered to act in a lawful way. She was shown here as being a little in fault in the community. She decided that she would say nothing and wait. People would forget the fault sooner and blame her the less if little were said. It was morning, Friday, the twentieth of June. She went about the affairs of her house, diligent of them. The mornings were long, since daylight came early, and she had much time for these appearances and decisions. By eleven o'clock she had settled to a fixed mood or opinion. Cundy had not come to accuse her or to roar out his wrath at his daughter in her presence. He stayed away because he was afraid of what she would say to him and afraid of the state of mind he would carry away from her house. She would stay quietly at home and say little, she decided anew. She prepared the noon meal, holding to this opinion. Making a dish of tender peas with little white dumplings floating among them, she tasted the sauce carefully, entering into each fine savor, the butter, the salt, the blended odors of cooking peas and cream.

During the morning a swift shower fell. It pelted over the barnyard and made rivulets run down through the hen-yard and the wood lot, setting the little chips afloat. Andy took shelter in the barn, and looking from the kitchen window into the long bright lines of the falling water, Philly saw him standing within the barn door, and all the hens were huddled not far from his feet. The water would be running in a little shower again inside the hen-house. Seeing the hens all about him, Andy would know why they had not chosen their own house for shelter. She would let all be, unharried, for the present, being herself secret and careful.

In the afternoon the Shepherd young man came hallooing from the pasture. When he came inside the door Philly had a sudden awe of him, as if he were some other than what he claimed to be. He came talking about the guineas, making them a wonder, worth talking about.

"I reckon you know a right smart of Latin," Philly said. "You said your name was Shepherd. Is it John B., maybe?"

He said that he was called Ben and that he was at work at Stoner's farm. She had a swift picture of him as going in and out, as being up on the hill where the wheat was harvested. He talked of the house-painter, Grove, and made him out a liar, and she had a new fear because the painter was proved now a lying villain.

The boy was a thin strong youth sitting on one of the chairs not far from the mantel. Philly could hear old John B. telling the names of things in Latin and making a long flow of singing words in

this hidden speech. All at once she wished he
were gone. Her creeping fear of him grew while
he sat in her room. His head, outlined against
the boards above the fireplace, seemed to be fixed,
as if it could not move, as if it had never moved.
It seemed impossible for him to move. He was
sitting within two feet of the stone under which
the treasure was buried, but the stone was covered
by the chest. His feet were near the neighboring
stones that were exactly like the stone that hid the
kettle. He seemed never to have moved, as if he
were fixed there forever. His name was Shepherd,
John B., and he had been living forever. "They
call me Ben," he said. It was no matter what they
called him. She leaned forward and said, almost
whispering: "Didn't you live out there?" pointing
lightly toward the north, toward the graveyard.

"Yes," he said, "yes, ma'am."

She had known it. She asked again.

"What was it drove you in?"

"It was the ants."

"What ants?"

"These little black ants and red ones. They're
everywhere underground. You'd be surprised to
see how many, if you've never taken notice of how
they run through the ground. They're under every
foot of the earth around in these parts."

"They get into my milk-house sometimes," she said. "Or iffen I happen to have a little piece of meat out there. A ham I put out there once."

"They're sure to get any meat that's in their way. They've got a keen scent after flesh. They must have had a colony right under the place where I slept."

"Did you sleep long?" she asked. She became more fearful and she moved toward the door thinking it would be better to go.

"Long? What makes you ask that? Long? I almost always slept until I heard a farm bell ring."

"Whose farm bell?"

"Yours. The one with the high tone, 'bing-bing bing-bing.' Then I'd say, 'It's time to outwit the ants.' . . ."

Philly went without the door and she walked about the kitchen, wondering what she had best do next. When she had lingered for a little she peeped into the parlor door to see if the appearance had gone, but it sat on the chair beside the hearth. It was faced forward, as if it looked at some object straight before its eyes, but she could not believe that it was seeing now. She rattled the wood in the kindling box and made a noise with the tinware on the table, looking then in at the door to see if the charm were cast and the appari-

tion gone. She went outside to the well and drew
a bucket of fresh water, and she began to drink a
cup of it. While she was busy thus the creature
came from the house and stood not far away on
the stones before the kitchen door.

"I have to go gather the guinea eggs," she called
out. She took a pan and a long spoon from a shelf
and started off toward the barn lot and the thicket.
"Nobody can go with me," she called back. She
hurried when she had passed beyond the tulip tree
and she hid herself in the tall bushes farther away.
Looking out from her hiding she saw Shepherd
climb over the stile into the pasture and later she
saw him striding over the brow of the pasture rise,
going quickly as if he were going to the schoolhouse to call her to books.

She was afraid to return to the house until she
saw Andy coming from the field. He seemed troubled, listening, asking her to listen, but he did not
ask after the visitor and Philly wondered if he had
seen it. She was quiet on her part, considering
these matters again. Perhaps Andy had not seen
the creature although it had walked before him as
it entered the house. He sat looking hard at the
wall, in a dream. Then he brought some heavy
weights, iron bolts and smoothing irons, and he
laid them in the lower drawer of the chest that

covered the hearthstone. He locked the drawer afterward, and thus he added great weight to the chest that protected the stone.

Philly sat indoors, above-stairs by the north window all of an afternoon and patched bits of bright rag together, and cut squares and triangles of cloth, to make a quilt. The apparition of the day before still troubled her, but the quilt was a consolation, an old pleasure. She herself had a Shepherd ancestress somewhere far back, but whether the name was Kitty or Polly, she could not now remember. All this was very long ago, as she viewed the earth. It was a terror to her that her farm bell should be waking the dead in the old Shepherd burying-place. This too was a matter to be hushed away and forgotten. In the night she had felt again for the two pearls that should have been swinging from Andy's trunk, but they were not there nor were they in any part of the house. She sewed the seams with small neat stitches and creased them flat. The shapes of the design appeared through the sewing and the pattern came free of the sorts and kinds.

She heard Andy, at the middle of the afternoon, making a noise below, as if he were through with

his work in the field and would like now to see
the kitchen set for supper. She liked better to work
with the bits of cloth, ginghams and calicoes, little
triangular snips of one sewed beside a triangular
snip of another, a rag beside a rag, and all the girls
and boys of the countryside were in and out of
mind, floating back and coming forward. "I
couldn't be the one to manage whe'r they marry
or not," she said. "I've got enough of my own to
manage." Threading the needle was the difficult
part. The eye would double, making two, and
then go out altogether. She would try many times
before the thread was securely put through the
little opening, but when it hung lightly there and
would not float away in her hands, she would relax
her deeper care and bend again to the scraps, the
needle safely held in her mouth. She remembered
the star pattern that Susie always liked and she
blended Susie with the girls that stood off among
the fields and talked with them and about them,
all in one breath. Susie had grand-daughters somewhere; they were all full of their own matters;
and Susie was dead, too, she reflected, but she put
this aside. She could not worry herself about that.

"You can't take notice to that-there, neither,"
she said.

She had never taken much notice of the fact of

Susie's death. Susie and the girls were together in her thought. She remembered too that Susie had liked to wear a part in her hair, a little white line running down through the dark of her head, and that Imogene wore a part too, and so also did Bonnie.

All at once a clear thing stood straight across all the pictures of her mind and spread widely. She saw it from a long way off, but it had once been near at hand, it had once been her own to have and to know. She viewed it as an onlooker, seeing it in her own life and in the girls, blurred and moving, floating out of view and coming back with a quick beating of her heart and her breath. It was something the girls had every day; it was a common thing with them, to be talked about when they were together. It was gone then from her mind and she could not name what it had been.

She looked intently at the small seam she had been stitching, a light and a dark piece being sewed together, the needle making little beating movements between the threads. The taste of the thread was in her mouth where the needle had lately been. Then whatever had been vividly spread through her thought but a moment before came back. It was a knowledge of herself as being

lovely both without and within, as having inside
herself a warm flow of blood and little tremors of
delight. Delight was beautiful and she had a fine
measure of it inside herself somewhere and everywhere. Andy was near her to make her know how
lovely she was. He wanted her in his house. He
had but little to say; there was not much to tell.
It was something they had all kept together, it was
in all equally. It was dim now in the knotting of
a thread. It was seen a long way off, departing. She
could not say clearly what it had been. She did not
know what she had been thinking about.

She had not heard Andy below for a long time
now, and a vague fear began to grow, as if it took
a beginning at the top of her head and spread
downward. It was a fear that Andy might leave
her, that she might go forward in life alone, that
he might have taken a part of what was in the kettle and gone away. She knew that he would not
take all, that his hard and just feeling would require that her part would be allowed. She saw her
life spread before her in desolation, the farm
empty of life, sunk under the hard, sterile rock of
the earth. Her breath came in short catches and a
stiffness spread through her chest. She pushed the
needle into the cloth, making small stitches, being
vividly alive only where her fingers beat up and

down at the seam. He might go, she contrived, he might have already gone. He might have left the whole of the kettle, not wanting the burden of it. Her breath was quiet and still.

A low sound below, a drawing of a chair over the floor or the settling of a footstep, and she knew that he was still there. Her fear seemed somehow petty and pretty in the face of these accustomed sounds.

She remembered that Susie always liked to name the pieces of her quilt, and she went back to the patterns Susie liked to make. "I'll name this-here Imogene," she muttered, choosing a favored bit of cloth with small bright flowers on a wan ground. She became warm in anger as she told the whole story of Cundy's meanness. When Andy came back again to make a rumble and a clatter she remembered that it was her duty to go below and provide him with food.

"It's the longest day in the year," Andy said. He was coming into the kitchen door with the pails of milk. "And I can very well believe it, what they tell. Daylight lasts away into the night now. Even past seven o'clock you can still see to read a paper outside without a lamp."

He lowered himself to a chair and began to talk of the fine crop of hay. "I'm of a mind to start work on a new roof to the hen-house a Monday," he said. "I looked around today and for a fact the hen-house does need a roof the worst sort."

"It's three years late you looked around," Philly said, "but no matter. I'd want the roof built so the water can run off both ends iffen it wanted to. I'd best go out and show what kind I want."

In the hen-yard the fowls had gone to roost in the great tulip tree, the perch they habitually used in summer. Philly pointed here and there, making clear the needs of the hens, and she climbed to the top of the pig-house, calling Andy to come after her, that she might show him the shape of the roof she desired. Andy climbed stiffly after her and they stood thus pointing and arguing over the roof until they came at last to harmony over it. He said that he would get a master carpenter to fit the roof and he would not stint the cost. They stood on the top of the pig-house almost a half hour and the twilight gathered, the fading sunlight yielding slowly to the rising moon.

They came slowly back to the house and went slowly indoors and into the deeper twilight of the parlor. Then Philly flung up her arms over her head and screamed twice, scarcely aware as yet of the cause that had brought the volley from her throat. She saw an upturned stone and a litter of yellow earth on the floor. She saw then a vacant world stretched out in all ways, as if the walls of the house and all the air and the ground were taken away. The pot of money was gone. She ran to the hearth and looked into the hole, seeing the trace which the kettle had made as it rested on the packed clay. The print of the iron pot was still faintly marked in a round groove. A kettle had been there. But there was nothing of a mark or sign to show what way it had gone.

She cried out her distress over and over, beating her hands together, and she pointed into the hole, calling Andy to make clear to him what had happened. She sat in her chair and rocked back and forth, in a state of grief and rage. Andy examined the hearthstone and he shook his head, saying, "I had a suspicion. I had a suspicion there might be robbers in the country." He trembled as he stood over the empty hole, which seemed small in size now that the pot was gone out of it. He walked the floor, trembling, and his legs shook as he stepped forward, but he did not cry out nor beat the air with his arms. Philly cried and grieved, reciting her wrongs and her losses.

"We'll never see a sight of it again," she said.

"We'll never. You could go out after the robbers iffen you'd stir yourself. . . . I'll never again see a pot full of gold while life lasts."

When she pictured the kettle clearly she burst into fresh grief. Remembering the bright coins in the pot, and how she had scoured each one to make it bright, she leaned forward, her tears gathering anew, and her throat seemed turned within to a liquid stream of sad complaint that came out of her without her assistance. Outside the light had scarcely changed, and a mockingbird was singing. Philly walked to the hearth and looked into the empty pocket of earth again, and she broke into a low spent wailing, sinking back then to her chair. Andy lit the lamp on the mantel and held it near to the vacant hole to examine there more closely. Philly was crying out her distress.

"I'll never see such a sight again while life lasts. I'm a poor old woman withouten so much as a piece of silver or a piece of gold to buy a little comfort for myself. . . . Ne'er a thing to give to another. I'm ugly, as withered and thin, as ugly as any you'd ever meet on the road. God knows, how ugly and old and withered and done-for I am!"

They were still then, Andy listening to the sounds outside. "Can you hear?" he'd say, whispering. "Hearken, Philly, can you hear a step in the grass?" The house was empty of every other sound and empty of any purpose. The twilight seemed hard and fixed, empty of rest, shed of all sweetness.

"A half hour ago they came here," he said, bending at the hearth and listening. "They're not gone far. . . . They might be outside now. . . . Philly, can you hear steps . . . in the grass?"

The household pieces stood about the wall, the dresser, the organ, the sofa, a chair, the high chest pushed away from the hearth by the robber, and they seemed to keep together a treachery, for they had been present when the thief came to lift the stone. Grief flowed easily from her eyes and from her throat.

"It was such a pretty kettle, filled up to the top," she cried, whispering the words after her shaking voice had moaned softly, or again:

"I'm some old crooked woman that lives in a poor old torn-down house. And Susie and all the rest are dead. . . . Oh, God's pity on me! I've lived a hundred years already. . . . And I'll live a hundred more, old . . . and life is hard-to-get . . . hard to keep . . . hard to get shed of. . . . No need to think again about the pretty part . . . weddens and a bright dress for a girl to wear

. . . yourself or any other. . . . Oh, God's own pity on me! No little pleasure for myself and ne'er a thing to give to any other. . . . I'm as poor as ever I was, and poorer. . . . We are a poor old man and woman, poor together. . . . Oh, how poor I am!"

"You're in too big a hurry," Andy said. He was standing by the door, looking out, but he turned back to her. "No place is a safe place to talk in, and you talk too long sometimes, and talk too much. Why can't you hold still for a little spell?"

She could feel a great stillness gathering within herself, and a vast emptiness without. She broke into a newer wail and moaned without speech, rocking forward and back.

"Don't take on, Philly, and don't worry yourself any more," Andy said. He urged stillness upon her, for he was still now. "Wait till you hear what's to tell," he said. "You are ahead of yourself with worry, seems like."

He went outside cautiously, a step or two steps at a time, and he walked about, stooping to look into the shadowed hedges. He went entirely around the house, his feet striking unevenly at the stones by the well and beating again in the grass at the farther side of the yard. When he came back presently he walked with ease, as if he had satisfied himself that no one lurked near the house. Philly sat staring at the empty place where the kettle had been, weary now, but she did not cry aloud again. Then Andy went to the mantel shelf above the fireplace and he opened the door of the clock to look carefully inside. When he had peered enough to satisfy himself that there was something within he thrust in his fingers beyond the pendulum and brought out a bright gold coin, and he held it out toward her. Philly saw the bright piece with amazement, and she walked over to stand beside him, taking the coin slowly into her hand.

"It's to buy a roof to the hen-house," he said. "You can have all of it. It'll buy the roof and a little more."

She made a great clatter over the coin. She looked at it closely and laughed over it, or she held it toward the door where the light made it more yellow. She broke into indetermined cries, saying no sensible thing, but making a clattering laughter that became speech as it told of her joy and her restored pride in life. When she had cried out and laughed over the coin until she was satisfied with it she came back to the hearth and held out her

hand for another. Andy thrust his fingers into the
clock and brought out a piece of silver for her.
She laughed over the two pieces, and she came
back again, asking:

"Some chinaware for Imogene," she said. "I
promised myself I'd favor Imogene when she came
to her wedden. Some china dishes, I want, for
Imogene." She held up her hand for more.

Then Andy reached into the clock again and
brought out another bright gold piece and gave
this without delay. She took it off the end of his
lean knotty fingers and put it with the other coins,
crying out with a new joy, bubbling and breaking
within until her words and her gentle laughter
mingled together and twittered as if a flock of
some pleasant birds were in her throat. While she
was thus jabbering laughter, standing beside the
overturned stone, holding the coins, first one and
then another up to the light, Andy reached again
into the clock and probed there, driving his fingers
more deeply into the cavern, keeping free of the
weights as he searched for some last piece. Philly
left off her chittering to watch what he did. Then
he brought forth the last piece and gave it across
to her quickly, thrusting it hurriedly as if he
would not allow a change of mind to interfere
with it.

"For the Lord," whispering. "Give this-here to the Lord, I say. Philly, to the Lord."

Philly took the last coin, a gold piece of equal value with the other ones, and she burst into a new flower of joy over it, breaking into laughter that interfered with her words and made of them a gentle twittering and a musical guttural like the pleased cries of some small birds flying over a full meadow. She walked to the door to examine all in the fading daylight, and there the gold shone with a dark luster but the silver was less bright. She held up each coin, naming what each would buy and saying where each would go.

Andy turned about, and he went out at the back door of the house. Philly went after him when she had knotted the four coins into a handkerchief and hidden them in her bosom. He seemed to be looking for the small black calf that was always straying, and he walked about over the pasture where the light of the day had passed into the brilliant light of the moon. When he came to a stile that mounted over a fence at the side of his hay field he stopped to rest and he sat on the stile, high on the brow of the farm, in the bright light.

"I had a suspicion there were robbers in the

country," he said, "and I had a right suspicion. No place is fitten to talk in when robbers are about."

"And so you, I reckon, took out the kettle yourself today whilst I sewed on the quilt, and you hid it in another place. Before the robbers came, I reckon."

"It wouldn't be safe to name where I hid the pot, Philly. But I can make known to you where 'tis."

"Yes."

"You recollect a time I said I couldn't cut down a certain old walnut tree because it would be bound to fall on a pear tree and break the top? That pear tree is the right tree, Philly, but don't you ever name the name of it inside the house, you hear what I say, or call it out in anger."

"No."

"And whenever I open the pot to take out," he whispered, "I'll remember to take out a piece for the Lord. Recall it to my mind iffen ever I forget, Philly. Recall it to my mind how I stood, my hand up in the air for a strong oath, iffen ever the kettle is opened and some is taken out, one piece of equal kind goes to God. Make me recollect I promised."

"I'll recall it to your mind, Andy, yes. But I won't pledge to make you do what I recall. I'll do all I can to hold you to the words of your oath, but I won't engage to make you want to do it or to make you give the gold. The ways of mankind are past finden out and strange, they are. I'll make you recollect your vow and recollect how the robbers came too late and your kettle was saved, for the time anyway, but whe'r you give the gold is in the hands of God, I reckon."

They sat on the stile in silence, thinking of what Philly had just said. Then Andy said that the little black calf was out of the pen and that he had better find her before he went to the house. She was a troublesome calf, he said, always jumping over the fence and running off to the pasture. He was afraid she might make a way into the hay field and founder herself on the stubble. He thought that he saw her off in the bushes beyond the place where the old work-horse was grazing, and after he had rested a short while longer he would go to fetch her home, he said. The evening had slipped into the brightly lit night and the moon stood large and round in the pale blue of the sky. He spoke again of the calf and said she was a care and burden and would be, he supposed, until she got herself a calf. He had said this of the black heifer before, many times over. When he had peered again toward the bushes he was assured that she was quietly grazing there, still on the pasture side of the fence. He went back to speak again of the robbers and to say he had a suspicion who they were and that he wouldn't dare go near the place where the kettle was buried while they went at large, although he had covered the place so that it looked as if it had never been disturbed.

"Then," Philly said, "the pearls, the two fine precious little stones that came with the kettle. I never named it to you before, but what, I might as well know, what went with the stones?"

"I took the pearls outen the kettle," he said.

"Well, yes, you took out the pearls . . ."

"I hid the pearls someplace near at hand. It happened, though, I loaned the pearls to somebody over a night, and it was two nights or three before they came back. . . . I thought I heard a noise. Did the black heifer jump the fence, Philly?"

The little heifer had not jumped over the fence. She was nosing quietly about in the brush to find a bit of tender green on which the sun had not shone. Andy had loaned the pearls to somebody, as she had supposed, had given them out of his hands. Sitting on the stile, waiting to take the calf home, he seemed scarcely to know that the pearls had been away from him and he did not know how great a risk he had made for the stones when he let some other admire them and want them. Andy was of such a temper as would hold fast to one coin or a few, but aroused by some unaccustomed emotion, he would easily give everything. Guessing who the borrower of the pearls might have been, she let him talk for a little about his fear of the robbers, and she asked then suddenly:

"Was it Hester Trigg, maybe? The one you loaned the pearls, was it Hester?"

"It was Joe Trigg's widow, yes. How it was we talked about the pearls firstplace was this. She showed me a queer piece of rock she'd found on the low side of a field and asked me what kind 'twas. It was a stone with marks in rings all over it. I passed her on the road whilst I was on my way to the shop with the mower."

The kettle being safely hidden and the thieves thwarted, it was no great matter to her now that Andy had let the pearls go for a little while. She watched the black calf as it passed into the shade of the brush and made there a more dense shadow, and she thought with delight of the saved kettle and the four coins tied now into a little hard lump within her bosom. Andy had given her all that he had put in the clock, had yielded the last coin. These pieces would buy what she most desired, for herself and Imogene, but one piece would go for charity. Andy had not known the charm and the cunning that had kept the pearls out of his hands for two or three days.

"I won't lay me down to sleep in comfort until I know those robbers are out of the country," he said. "I won't rest easy till I know."

"How did you tell it you got the pearls first-place?" Philly asked. "How did you tell Hester you came by the pearls?"

"I didn't say. I asked would she care to see what a fine stone a pearl is. But the pearls are back now where I kept the sack before ever I loaned them out. It was Friday I told her she could keep the pearls another night and try them for ear-bobs against her face, as she desired."

Hester had begun with quietness and good sense, intent on the strange ways of stones. But presently she was keeping the stones another night to try them for ear-bobs. Philly could see Hester by the light of two bright lamps trying the pearls, having them fastened somehow to her ears.

"And then today, what?" she asked.

"Today I went there, passed on my way to the

shop to get the mower. I had a suspicion about robbers in the land and I didn't care iffen she kept the pearls longer. When I got there she was out by the beehives to talk to somebody a right smart while. I had the mower, and the mules didn't want to stand, and so she came. She gave the pearls back to me. She hurried out where I stood and gave me the little sack. That was all there was to that-there. The pearls are back where I hid them firstplace. Not in the kettle, you understand."

"The man over against the beehives, the man that drove the want for your two pearls out of Hester's head, I reckon that was Lester Rudds. Come to buy a little honey to sweeten his bread. Was it?"

"No, it wasn't Lester, and anyhow the honey is not ready to take yet. It was Sam Cundy. Sam Cundy it was."

"Sam Cundy! That's a good piece of news to hear. And he was in a ragen way, I reckon, his hands up in the air and his fists clenched. Did he curse Imogene and make a threat to kill? Sam Cundy would be enough to stop the bees in their work and drive the swarms up into the sky, iffen he's in a mad way, in the ragen way he was the fore part of the week. I'd hate to go in amongst a parcel of bees with Sam Cundy, iffen he's like he was on Sunday last. How was Sam and what did he say?"

"He didn't say much I could hear, but my ears are not a sharp kind, as you well know. His hands were down and iffen I recollect right they were inside his pockets. He had a rested look, like a man that's well content."

"You surely made out to know what they talked about whilst you waited for Hester to bring your pearls you loaned her to keep safe for a spell. From the look on her face you could tell what was in their talk, maybe."

"I couldn't hear much was said, but from the little I heard and the looks on Hester and Sam I made out they were talken about the bees and what kind is the best and she'd point out a hive and say, 'This lot is a master hand to make honey. Italian bees, they are,' or again she'd say 'a little black bee,' or 'corn-tassel honey is my favorite honey.' I heard him say once, 'Bees kept near a clover field.' That was all I made out from their talk."

The little black heifer came out of the brush into the open pasture and went slowly across the moonlit space. She was no longer an anxiety while she grazed in the open and drifted down toward

the feeding pen. The light in the small glade
where the calf had been seemed broken into parts
that crackled and spun, that drifted and glided in
streams, that came to an end each moment and
began again in some new drifting of the birch
leaves that blended with the white light. A mockingbird began to sing on the top of a high bough
and it pushed song up into the wide, lit sky with
a passionate throat, mounting and throbbing in
the beginning of a song frenzy that turned and
quavered, that asked and answered, that trilled
and bubbled and ended at length with a slow
hush-note. Then Philly knew that something
which had seemed to be a part of the quick, sudden, intermittent moonlight that lit the glade, was
the noise of speaking voices, as if people were
walking together, of people shouting and singing,
coming nearer. A drift of floating objects began to
form at the end of the pasture, three becoming
one and then turning to four, to be one and then
three, receding and coming forward. Imogene
came first into form and Giles followed soon after,
with a circle of girls and boys around, and Rudds
and his wife were quickly at hand, and Eliza
White and old Mr. Bonnie, with two of the
Roundtrees, walking up out of the powdered
air.

They came, driving the little black calf before them aimlessly, coming lightly forward, and Philly hailed them at the moment that they saw her on the stile with Andy. It was hello and whoo-pee, and a great wonder to see who would be out here in the pasture in the moonlight, it as bright as day. Giles and Imogene had been invited to Rudds's house for supper, and a group of others, the most of them young boys and girls, had come bringing presents of kitchenware.

"I said, while we're so near Cousin Philly we'll just walk over and say howdy-do," Imogene shouted lightly near to Philly's ear while the din of the gathering tinkled and clattered all about. The boys and girls romped over the pasture, pulling this one and that here and there, and Philly left the stile, Andy following, and they turned all, about and about, in the clear light.

Philly wanted to ask Imogene if she were married in a way to please all and if she had made another wedding, but she delayed asking because the question condemned the first wedding and her own part in it. She thought that presently she would take Giles aside and lead him to talk of it, but the minutes ran past and the delay seemed easier to perform, and she thought that if she were quiet and asked nothing, by and by the true way of it would be made clear. She would sit quietly by and let the truth appear.

The light of the moon was almost as bright as the day and Philly could not be sure that the twilight had gone. Bonnie's dress caught the light and flashed a newer yellow, and all the girls were pleased with the new beauty the moon had brought to their clothing; and they made their skirts dart and flutter in and out of the bright glow to feel themselves a part of the flashing color and to know that they were lovely. The throng, set in a circle, made a great wheel that turned about a little thorn bush and sang a game-song:

> Here we go round the mulberry bush
> On a cold frosty morning . . .

When this was sung once through another song arose from another part of the wheel, all the boys and girls catching hands and turning, and Philly and Andy, caught in the whirl, stepped with the rest.

"We'll play drop-the-handkerchief," they said, one speaking and all acquiescing. Bonnie rolled a kerchief into a tight ball and flung it high into the air so that one might catch it. That one would be the first to run about the ring and drop the gift behind someone's heels.

They joined hands, all in a ring again, and the great wheel began to turn, spread wide to make a moving circle, singing the rhyme of the mulberry bush. The great wheel turned, making ready a world, a world of mankind turning all together, Philly and Andy and Ronnie Rudds and old Bonnie, with all the girls and boys of the farms. As the earth itself the wheel turned under the moon, singing, but after a little while it came to a stand, and Ed Sims, who had caught the knot of linen Bonnie had tossed into the air, was the first to run about it. He went about the circle twice, and when he had passed Philly's place the second time, the boys and girls flung up their arms and clapped their hands because Philly had not taken up the prize and run with it. She had not thought that Sims or any other would give her a gift. She must go to the middle of the ring and wait until she should be redeemed. The great world was turning again, the girls and the boys making a song out of the couplet of the mulberry bush and the frosty morning. Philly sat on the ground and let the great wheel roll about her.

The black calf came close to the game in a still moment, but it ran away in fright when the wheel began to turn. The boys and girls were giving the prize swiftly from one to another and running swiftly about the great circle. Sims gave it to Bonnie who ran him to a place and gave it then to Giles, and the giving ran forward, the girls favoring the boys, and the boys the girls, but Ronnie Rudds was put into the middle and presently Andy came too, and Eliza White, because she could not run fast enough to escape the little linen ball when it was thrown. The great wheel was turning; although these were put out of it, it still moved without them, and the song of the mulberry bush ran perversely above the warm moonlit pasture. Philly leaned toward Eliza to speak with her privately.

She wanted to ask if Giles and Imogene were married, if they were married again, another time, or if one time were enough. "Are Giles and Imogene married now? Or what happened?" she wanted to ask, and she leaned forward with this speech ready at the edge of her lips. But the question seemed wrong, as being somehow too early or too late, and she thought that she would wait a little and let the answer come to her in its own way.

Instead of these questions then, having leaned near to Ronnie and Eliza, she said:

"They say it's the longest day in the year, midsummer day, and I can very well believe what they tell. It's long a-plenty. Summer is a warm season and pleasant. I just love summer."

"It's hard to recollect how cold it once was," Ronnie said, "but it was cold though."

"I'm afeared we might have a cold winter, after the summer so warm."

"Oh, I'm afraid so too."

"And wood so hard to get, and coal so far to haul."

"The dark days. And night settled down soon after four o'clock."

"You don't seem to take any notice to yourself, or any interest, and it don't seem worth while to do anything beyond what you're bound to."

"When the work is done you say to yourself, 'What'll I do now anyway?'"

"You just aim to get through the day, and then the next day comes. You get out a few carpet rags to tack, but hit's too dark to see, and you just sit down and wait till hit's time to light the lamps."

"But it's a long time off yet till winter. You can recall the dark days, night on hand early, but it's hard to recollect the cold."

"It's a misery it's hard to recollect after it's gone. . . ."

Were Giles and Imogene married? Philly

wanted to ask this of someone, but she could not find a pretty way to fit it into words and she let it wait to find its own reply. Giles and Imogene were caught now into the fury of the game, for all the young men delighted in giving to Imogene and they were continually tossing the little ball behind her heels. The girls were giving their prize to the boys who in turn gave to the girls, this way and that, and they chased each other around and around on the outer rim of the world, or the great wheel would be turning, making ready. While they were singing again, catching hands to make a new circle when the old one had become broken and sloven, two men came out of the powdered air at the edge of the field where the little thicket began. They came slowly into the open field, walking aslant with the great turning wheel, and Philly saw that they were the two painters. They sat on the ground as if they would stay awhile and watch the merry-making, and Philly had a fear of them, remembering now the overturned stone.

"I've got a suspicion the country's full of robbers," Andy said.

"Robbers? Has somebody lost?" Ronnie asked.

"I'd be afeared almost to go home tonight, with so many strangers all about. I'm of a mind to stay out here all night."

"Hear Andy Blair talk. Suspicious, I always said he was. . . ."

"I've got evidence there's robbers in the land . . . it's no new thing, surely . . . robbers fitten for a prison sentence. . . . A man's house was entered . . . was it today or a long while back? . . ." They were talking in whispers or in low throaty grunts of fear and caution.

The game broke apart and the men began to try their skill at calling home the farm stock, making a contest such as was tried at the County Fair. Practicing their call-cries and each trying to out-do the others, they stood in a line and let the girls judge them. Luke Rudds was calling home the pigs, crying "hoo-ee, hoo-ee, peeg, peeg, peeg, peeg." The great free cry went across the pasture, and next Lester Rudds, Luke's father, took up the contest and called in his way, flinging out another, "hoo-ee, peeg, peeg," which was more sonorous than the other's but did not last so long, for the younger man had a greater endurance.

Then Ed Sims began his cry, tearing the night apart with a widely flung, deep-chested, sonorous, "hoo-ee, peeg, peeg," and Philly leaned suddenly near to Ronnie Rudds and asked:

"What took a-hold of Hez Turner and made him act like he did, made him run off so fast?" It seemed a light question as it passed her lips, scarcely bearing on anything. "What made him?"

"It was Sam Cundy. Sam Cundy intimidated Turner and drove him away before he had time to fill in the last part of the document. He's back now and it's all filled in and sent to the Clerk."

"It turned out he was qualified a-plenty, unknown to all, I reckon," Philly murmured. "He was qualified the same as any other." It was a satisfying thought to her and she sat back in her place to enjoy the ease it brought to her. Ed Sims was still calling the pigs, out-doing Luke at his best, putting command and entreaty and promise into the call. "Hoo-ee," to rouse the swine to attention, and "peeg, peeg, peeg," to entice them and command.

"If I heard that, I'd come, whe'r I was a pig or not," a girl cried out.

"Now it's turkeys. Call home the turkeys."

"It's time to call in the turkeys."

Luke Rudds went first in this, flinging out a thin high "pee-pee-pee, pee-o-wee" that went higher and more high until the limits of his voice were reached. Lester Rudds and Giles followed, calling the same, and Ed Sims, when his turn

came, flung out a high, rough cry that made the
girls shout, for they said he would frighten the
turkeys back into the briars if ever they had
taken a notion to come at the calls of the other
men.

"Oh, call the horses, call the horses home. Leave
the turkeys to the women."

They were practicing at their voices, all together, without order. Rudds called them to quiet
and gave Giles the first turn. Then a wide "coulp
—coulp—coulp" went across the hill, sufficient to
wake the horses if they slept in the warm pastures
and set them running toward their barns and their
bridles. The cry was followed by a high shrill
whistle from Wilson's lips where his two fingers
were fitted under his tongue. Then the elder
Rudds, his cry less loud and insistent, as sufficient
only to call home those that had not strayed far,
although he tried again and again; but Luke
leaped into the contest with his great shrill whistle,
made with finger and thumb, a hard wild shrill
call that seemed to search the sky if there were any
horses there, that seemed to go straight up to the
moon. Ed Sims squared his broad shoulders, Luke
being done, and flung out a deep "coulp—coulp—
coulp" with the whistle following, less shrill than
Luke's but more deep and searching, as if the dark

under the earth would be searched and the cavern horses called together.

The girls were crying out their laughter and calling Luke to enter the contest again. Philly leaned near to Eliza to speak with her privately and she asked:

"Who put it in Cundy's head to let Turner come back to fill in the papers? How was it Cundy ever let Turner come here?"

"Who? I wouldn't say. But I think it might 'a' been somebody that could make him see it in a smooth way. Made him stop his threats at Turner. . . ."

Philly waited a little, to seem in thought over this matter. Then she leaned forward to ask again:

"Was it Hester Trigg? Was it Hester, do you reckon?"

"I came past Hester's gate today whilst I was on my way home, and I see a stout roan horse hitched to her gate. I see Sam Cundy over amongst the bees, easy in his ways, and you'd think he went there to get a little honey to sweeten his bread tomorrow."

Ronnie Rudds had heard what was being said. She leaned into the close knot of whisperers and whispered in her turn:

"Anyway, it was Hester that told us we could

send word to Turner. Said he could come back now and fill in the paper. It was Hester spread the news it was a wedden after all, and all the old bygones would be let be."

The men were calling the horses still, for they took a delight in this and they learned of one another. "Coulp—coulp—coulp" went again and again across the pastures and the younger Rudds was piercing the air and the sky with his hard whistle, made with a finger and thumb under his bent tongue. Then the boys and girls were calling again for their game and they caught hands and swung the great circle wide, singing again. They flung a great circle, so wide this time that it spread about all who sat on the ground, about Philly and Ronnie Rudds and Eliza White and Andy as these sat together, and about the two house-painters, Larkin and Grove, who sat apart. The painters were now sitting within the wide ring that wheeled and flung madly around, shouting its way about an imaginary bush on an imaginary frosty morning.

Three or four new-comers appeared out of the brightly powdered air. They were dark shapes in a mass that stepped on undetermined feet, but they lifted suddenly and fell into design, four men coming quickly forward. The players in the ring hailed them with shouts of delight, shouting greetings without calling a name, as "Come on, whoever you are!" but these men walked quickly into the midst of the boys and girls, breaking the ring without apology.

Chief among the new-comers was Bob Dragoo, the sheriff, and three men walked with him. He turned the great sweeping ring aside, moving quickly and roughly through the scattering girls, and he laid his hands on Grove. Two men held Grove while another drew his hands together and bound them with iron cuffs. Grove cursed at this interruption of his freedom, and the girls were crowding near or scattering away, the men standing close about. Larkin had leaped out of the throng and he was running away into the cornfield. His head was bent low over the corn that stood waist high, and he limped over the clods for a moment and went out of view altogether where the field drooped below the hill.

"Let that one go," Dragoo said. "I've got nothing against him. He won't come back."

"You've got not one thing against me neither," Grove said, cursing. "You can let me go. You've got the wrong man, sir." Becoming bland and persuasive, "You've made a mistake, sir. I'm not

your man. Grove's my name. I'm a house-painter.
Ask Mr. Stoner if I'm not a good painter and mind
my own business."

"You're a right good painter, they say," Dragoo
answered him. "Take a-hold on the other side,
John. Take a-hold, Ed Sims, I need you to help.
Bring him along. You're a good painter enough.
Got a-hold of you on the other side is a deputy
from Fayette County. He's got a warrant against
you in his pocket." They were going swiftly away
and they merged to be one thing, to go limping
and halting off into the far moonlight.

One of the men of the four stayed to talk, Sims
being gone to help with the prisoner. "Money
took out of a green teapot," he said. "Three
months back. Two hundred and seventy-odd dollars inside a green teapot. Careless old lady never
missed it till last week. It's said he left paint marks
and fingerprints on the side of a green teapot."
The man was answering their questions of fingerprints on a paint can. They gathered about him,
but he had told all that he knew and he went away
after the group that attended the prisoner. Those
on the pasture hill stood about in a turning throng
pointing and telling, talking, now one and now all
together.

"I had a suspicion there might be robbers in

the neighborhood," Andy said. "God be praised!"

"I had a suspicion too," Philly said after him.

"Who ever would think there'd be thieves and robbers in our country, with not a thing anyplace worth a robber's time to steal."

"It's lucky I locked up my hen-house. . . . He said a green teapot. . . . I read that piece in the paper myself. . . . It was a little piece away down in one corner. . . . It's lucky I didn't have my house painted. . . . And I laid out my spoons to scour only today. . . . I never did trust the way that man looked. . . . But he looked innocent enough, too. . . . It was a little piece away down in one corner, and it said two hundred and seventy dollars. . . . Hid in a green—he said teapot, I recollected it as a coffeepot. . . . I recollected it as a teapot myself. . . . God be praised! God be praised!"

The voices were fluttering and leaping over one another, or they fell away finally as the matter was talked through and there was nothing more to say of it. Then, again:

> Here we go round the mulberry bush,
> On a cold frosty morning . . .

Imogene and Giles had left the game and they were sitting beside Philly and Ronnie in the middle of the ring. They were promising to come the next day to her house, and Philly hinted lightly of something, remembering the coin which would buy for Imogene, but she dared not promise. The game went forward, for the boys and the girls were not through giving gifts to each other with the dropping of the little knot of linen. At the edge of the field in the clump of thorn trees a mocking-bird was singing now and then, calling in quick whistled cadences or bending the song about and about, this way and there, long and short, short and long, coming to a plaintive asking with one low repeated note, and flinging sadness away to fly up into the moonlight with a sudden chick-cherry, chee-o-wee, the song never repeating altogether what had gone before. From time to time the cocks stirred in the barnyards and they questioned the brightness of the night with alarm. Nightjars flew incessantly through the sky with opened mouths to drain the insects out of the air, and when they descended to a lower plane, there was the roll of a drum in their swiftly descending feathers. Through the fitful passions of the mockingbird and the constant labors of the nightjars, the cock-crows would break and moan slowly off to an ending.

"Day would come in a little while. Come on,

we'd best go now," some were calling out. "It must be near morning."

"It's hardly night yet! It's never got dark yet. No. It's not near to morning. . . ."

"Day is right here at us. We must go." They were breaking the game and calling the girls to go. Eliza began to talk of something she had heard and all were still to listen with her, crying, "What was it?" or "I don't hear one blessed thing." In the moment of quiet Philly had heard a sound, a katydid trying his tools, making ready for song. It sang one faint "did," as short and hard as a pin-prick. Listening, all of them quiet, some of them heard the faint "did" again.

"Hit's a katydid for sure."

"Hardly out yet. You couldn't count it."

They were still listening again, and there came another faint "did" from the grass.

"Next week he'll begin to say 'katy' in a weak, skinny way. Then by and by he'll get both together and come out with a big bold 'katydid,' but that's a right smart while off yet."

"Midsummer night, and I wouldn't want to be a-hearen a frost token already."

"You couldn't begin to count the six weeks on that-there weak little piddlen noise."

"I'd hope you didn't have to. Ask Lester Rudds

iffen he counts six weeks till frost on the first katydid noise, whatever 'tis."

"Not till he comes out with a for-sure 'katydid.'
Not till he gets it a-goen in a big way. I don't
begin to count on that little good-for-nothing 'did'
myself."

"It's curious, though."

"It's curious to think about."

"In the midst of the first harvest, before the
corn is much above knee high, midsummer night,
and hot weather all around us, and you hear the
first frost-sign of a frost-sign yet to come."

"Oh, God's sake, think of it."

"A sign that a frost-sign is bound to follow."

"Day comes at two o'clock now. In a little while
it would be day. We'd best go now. . . ."

The boys and the girls were made to give up
their games and were called to go. They were
leaving, two and two or in little groups. Giles and
Imogene were gone.

Philly and Andy started back homeward, down
the pasture, driving home the little black calf. The
bushes and the briars, the tree trunks and the little
saplings, were full of vague, unbodied lovers, and
off a little way in the shadows there were these,
just out of sight, whispering, under the stones,
behind the ditches, under the hummocks. They

were all gone from the moonlight and the hilltop.

"I had a suspicion there would be robbers abroad," Andy said.

"At large, you mean, Andy."

"I am a lucky man. Luck always seems to come my way. Every time I open the kettle and take out some, don't let me forget."

They drove the little calf down toward the barn, urging her this way and that. "You don't think she got too much clover, do you, Philly? Are her sides bloated, do you think? . . . I had a right suspicion too . . . Don't let me forget what I said, my hand up in the air. . . ."

They urged the black calf forward, Andy calling, "Make her come this way, here. . . . You never did know how to drive a calf, Philly . . . or e'er other thing. Always in too big a hurry. . . . That way, now . . . here . . . head off on yon side. Now she's set straight . . . easy up, and she's in."